THE QUEENS EMPIRE

PREFACE

There were a lot of cinemas about in Birmingham, as there were in most cities and towns, but as television came into its own it put the cinemas under a lot of pressure. Some nights they were empty, a lot of them were shut down and demolished, some turned into stores, and some into dance halls.

The fifties and sixties were a magical time for these dance halls, not only rock and roll but ballroom too. This is the story of one dance hall, The Queens Empire. Right in the middle of the city and everybody who was anybody went there.

This story tells about the comings and going of the characters who used the Queens for their pleasure. Some funny, some very sad, but it's the sixties and free love was in abundance.

There were dance competition's, dance classes, and dance rivalry. Some would say it was the best time of their lives, and for some it was, but not all stories had a good ending.

When a group of people are together for long periods of time things inevitably go wrong, tempers flare, bitchiness, and that's just the men. The women were much worse, and the staff at the Queens had their moments as well. It all falls into a fascinating story.

CHAPTER ONE

The Queens Empire started off as a cinema in the late thirties right up to the late fifties, early sixties, and was very popular and provided entertainment for all ages. This could be seen in the films they showed daily, Saturday mornings were for the kids, Saturday matinee was a must for all the kids, and it was full within minutes of it opening its doors, but some families couldn't afford the nine pence it cost to go in, so for those kids the cinema charged sixpence and they had to miss the first cartoon. However, everyone was happy. When television took over our lives it was the end for a lot of cinemas and a sad day for a lot of people. But, when these cinemas were turned into dance halls a lot more people were happy than sad, a whole new life opened up for them. The music scene was changing, rock and roll was the new thing for the young ones, and some of the old ones too, ballroom dancing took off in a big way. All these dance halls opening brought all sorts of people together, men met there wives there, women met their husbands, and most of their social life was spent at these dance halls.

Saturday was a big night for everyone, young and old. Some went to the pub, some to the bingo, yes, they had bingo then, but most went to the dance halls. Yes, Saturday nights were dance nights, best suits, best dresses, some left their weekly bath until Saturday, can't pull a bird smelling of sweat, can you?
In the bar everyone would look at the opposition. *His suit looks nice, her dress looks nice, oh look at her arse, look at her tits, look at his dick sticking out of his trousers! Is it real or something he's put down there to make him look bigger?*

Well, this is all the young bucks talked about (ok some old ones as well). All wanted to be top dogs, *I'm the best dressed, I'm the best looking*, and so on. You had your obligatory wallflower, every dance hall did. You've seen them standing at the back, not getting involved in things, just too shy but hoping someone would ask them to dance. You go over to her and ask for a dance, she looks at you, then at the floor saying "sorry, no thank you".
"Bloody hell, what have you come for? It's a bloody dance hall, come on doll lets move it!"
"Oh, ok just one dance then."
"You sure doll? don't want to push things but let yourself go! come on."
They hit the floor and bloody hell did they go for it. They danced for a solid hour none stop dance after dance, he said "doll shall we have a rest and a drink?"
"Yes, ok" she said, and off to the bar they went.
"Cheers!" he says, "oh yes", she says, he looks at her and says, "are you a virgin or not?"
"What?" she says, turning very, very red, "sorry" he says, "didn't know how to put it".
"What do you mean?" she says.
Oh, dear young love and all that, that's the theme for the night, pull or be pulled. This guy was to the point, no social skills at all, needless to say he went home on his own. All together now, ah.

The Queens was owned by Mecca, they spent a lot of money changing the cinemas into dance halls all around the country.
The Queens was regal, big chandeliers, plenty of seats, restaurant upstairs, two nice bars, one for a quiet drink the other full of posers and anyone with a story to tell. The stage was especially nice, lights surrounded it with

plenty of room for the dance bands and rock bands who had a lot of equipment. The dance floor was nice enormous and always full.

Monday nights were modern dance night. Tuesday was free and easy night, that's the residence band playing music of the day and every so often one of the crowd would get on stage and sing. Some were good, not all, but it was great fun. Wednesday was strictly ballroom, no rock, just ballroom. Thursday was just records with a DJ, well, there were two of them, Vince, and Sally. Vince would play the records with plenty of banter, Sally just sang and danced around the stage to each record. She was great to watch, sometimes she would get one of the guys off the dance floor onto the stage to dance with her. There was never a shortage of partners, yes Thursdays were good fun. Fridays and Saturdays were just bloody full-blown rock and roll. Dance contests, beauty contests, miss Queens Empire of the month, and full every night (where do they all come from?) Sundays, the Queens was shut. There were smaller halls open but most big dance halls were closed on Sundays.

Lunch times were a big hit as well, Monday to Friday 12- 2, Vince would play records none stop. The restaurant was open, plenty of folk in there, no booze at lunch times, mainly the younger set were there for lunch times. Some came in for a coffee and a quick dance, some just danced for an hour then back to work, it was mostly full all week.
Mondays and Thursdays between 2-15 and 4-30 was taken up by dance classes, mainly ballroom, they were run by a married couple, Bert, and Anne. After a few months it was just ballroom, and a dance team was

formed. They entered a lot of competitions in and around Birmingham, then as they got better, all around the Midlands. So, as you can see the Queens was a well-run dance hall.

Micky Taylor was the first manager of the Queens, he also managed the rock band Quasimodo and when they got big, he put all his time into managing them, but he really got the Queens on the map. So, when the present manager took over (Sammy Woon, but changed it to Alphonse Bouffant, he said it sounded better than Sam, and I'm running the biggest dance hall in town and that name is so me) things were really swinging and it wasn't hard to follow Micky's work.
Alphonse said, "please don't call me Al, Alphonse or Mr Bouffant, all upmarket", he was nice to everybody, well, to their face. He was truly professional, very smart, always immaculately dressed, clean white shirt every day, sometimes twice a day, black suit, trousers with the best crease you've ever seen, shoes polished to the point you could have shaved in them, his hair, yes, you've got it, bouffant. Not a hair out of place, wherever he was in the dance hall you felt his presence. Very witty, always got an answer for everything, not always the right one mind, and talked very posh. He was in his mid forties and had worked in some of London's top hotels and knew how to handle people, he got fed up with it and changed his career. He was not married but had plenty of girlfriends, one night one of his girlfriends came to the Queens as they often did (not at the same time) this night one got on to the stage and stopped everything dead, then through the mic said "Sammy, will you marry me?" well you could hear a pin drop. Everybody's looking around, *who's Sammy?* At the back of the room

Alphonse was mortified, *the bloody bitch what's she doing?*

"Oh, come on Sammy!" she shouts pointing at him, "you said I'm yours forever last night."

Alphonse stood there stony faced but not for long, stood next to him was one of the bar staff collecting glasses, Alphonse grabbed him, "right get down there and get her off the stage!" and whispered something in his ear, "ok no problem" said this guy and off he went down to the stage. On his way there he was slapped on the back, "go on then son, tell her yes!", everyone was clapping him and cheering him on, they all thought he was Sammy. At the stage he jumped up and went down on one knee and said "yes I will marry you" she looked at him in bewilderment as if to say *who the fuck are you?* He then picked her up and carried her off the stage to rapturous applause, he put her down and ran with her back to the bar where Alphonse was waiting.

The band had struck up again, so everyone was dancing and singing, the spotlight had gone off her, thank God. Alphonse took his girl to his office then ripped into her, "what the bloody hell are you playing at you bitch? you could have put me in a very funny position! I know what I said last night but listen kid, good and hard, what goes on outside the Queens stays outside, ok got it? And no more fucking Sammy, Alphonse if you please" throwing his head back.

The next few days Alphonse had some funny looks, most of the staff knew his name was Sammy, but had changed it to Alphonse, but from those who didn't there was quite a bit of whispering and pointing.

Steve, who ran the bar, asked the lad who had got Alphonse's bird off the stage what he'd said to him, "not a lot, get her off there and quick and do whatever it takes, and said there's a fiver in it for you and pushed a

fiver in my hand, no sooner said than done but said keep it to myself".
"Shouldn't have told me then should you" said Steve?
"Give us a quid to keep my gob shut", and held out his hand, "what?" said the lad "no chance".
"Oh yeah" says Steve "if you still want your job, give it to me now".
"You bastard" said the lad handing over the quid, then walked off shaking his head.

Steve was the bar manager his job was to make sure the stock was right, the tills added up every night, order new stock when needed, hire and fire staff, the full Monty. He was only answerable to Alphonse, he'd got a big head and a bigger gob, ex army sergeant and everything had to be just right, there were three tills behind the big bar and one in the small bar. Six staff served the big bar and two in the small bar, every night he would say, "you two, that till, and you two, that till, and the last two, that till!" just like a bloody sergeant major, so if there was a problem when cashing up, he could narrow it down to two of them. But he was a bastard, when he was checking the tills as he did every so often to see if they wanted any change, he would take £1 out of one of them and put it in his pocket. Some weeks he made ten to fifteen pounds, a lot of money then, so at the end of the night one till was always down and he would give the two staff who's till it was a good bollocking. He made sure he only took a pound, as if he took any more there would be an investigation by Alphonse, ten pound a week was not too bad to be missing considering the amount of cash they took every night, so not a lot was said by the accountant, well not yet anyway.
Steve was also a womaniser, and at every opportunity he would play away, his wife ran the restaurant, she knew

he was at it but couldn't catch him. She was also very fiery and took no shit off anybody, but very popular with the staff and customers, so she picked up on most things, and most things involved Steve.
Her name was Pamela, she was quite good looking, she met Steve in the army, they wanted to run a pub together, but this job came up at the Queens. The money was good, so they put the pub thing on hold. She had two waitresses working for her, Stella, and Sally. Stella was close to Pam, and they always had a good old gossip when things were a bit quiet. What Stella missed, Pam picked up on and vice versa. "Oh, I didn't know that", or "did she, the dirty cow!", or "well I never thought he was like that bloody poof!" and so on.
The customers also discussed their troubles with Pam, she was an agony aunt, always ready with advice and everyone loved her.

In the kitchen was one chef and two assistants, the chef was called Jeff, yes, Jeff the chef. Bill and Ken were the assistants. Jeff was ex navy and was very good at banging out the meals when the restaurant was busy, nothing too fancy but all good food, quick was the name of the game, but no microwave ovens then mate. The menu wasn't too fancy, steak and chips, egg and chips, fish and chips, prawn salad, soup, rice pudding, tea cakes that sort of thing, one night a week they had an Italian night and that was always full.
The restaurant had sixty mats or places, about sixteen tables, and when things got busy one of the bar staff helped with the waiting, most of the time it was Clark, a young man in his twenties, dark hair, sideburns and looked a bit foreign but was from Birmingham. He was gay, loved chatting to everyone and fussed over all the young ladies. He asked Pam many times if he could

work permanently in the restaurant as he didn't like Steve. Pam said Alphonse would have to be told and she didn't think he would agree, so to just carry on as he was. She said, "I'm so grateful for your help", when he moaned about Steve, she would just calm him down, she was a true professional and didn't get too involved. Steve was her husband after all.

So, life at the Queens was never dull, always something or someone going off, just one big story.

CHAPTER TWO

Bert and Anne ran the dance classes on Monday and Thursday afternoons, they were both great dancers, waltz, tango, foxtrot, quickstep, very good together and lovely people. They met some years ago at Margate when their parents took them on holiday, they loved to dance when they went on to the pier, that was the place most folks went. At the end of the pier was a pub which let kids in at lunch time, it had a guy who played the piano, and it was always a knees up.

Bert and Anne's favourite song was Bright and Breezy Free and Easy, when they got older, they would go there on their own for holidays, always the same time of the year and they always went to the pier, Bright and Breezy Free and Easy, they knew it backwards.

They were natural dancers and very enthusiastic, when old enough they got married. Where? Margate of course, and where did they have the reception? You got it, the bloody pier.

Bert worked at the local post office, it was quite a big place, part of the sorting office for all the mail in Birmingham. He worked shifts, nights or 6am-2pm, so when he and Anne took over the dance classes, he was able to be there most afternoons. Anne worked for her mom and dad, they had a shop just off the Bull Ring, it sold most things, general goods, fruit and veg, tinned food, washing powder, nick knacks, bread, and cakes, it was a good shop (most of them were then). All very friendly and nothing was too much trouble for them. Anne was a favourite with all the customers, so very sweet and hard working, her dad let her have time off to go to the Queens. She was nearly forty when her and Bert took over the dance classes, they lived just outside of the City Centre in a council house, it was very well kept, they didn't have any children, they were too busy said Anne (but not too busy for sex).

Bert was the force behind the ballroom dance classes, he asked Alphonse if he could start the classes as most of his friends were into ballroom dancing.
At first Alphonse wasn't too interested, he said to open the dance hall afternoons would cost too much, but Bert pointed out that the lunch time sessions were doing fine, and most days were full, so what's wrong with them having them? They would do their own music and just use the bottom end of the hall. "Anne and I want to get a team together so we can enter dance competitions and bring some fun to the dance hall, plus there are a lot of older folks who want this badly."
Alphonse said OK but he didn't want anything shabby, it had to be done very professionally. They were the best dance hall in the city and must keep their reputation intact. "Any crap and you're out".
"And if we do ok?" said Bert, "will you support us?"
"Of course, I will" said Alphonse, "but you have got to prove to me that it's worth doing."
They did, and they had the best dance group in the city, when you have two people with the drive Bert and Anne had you couldn't fail.

Monday just after the lunch time gig Bert and Anne stood there at the end of the dance floor, they knew some of their friends would turn up, but wanted a mix of young and older people. To get the right mix you need the right personalities, some older to give responsibility, and younger to give enthusiasm, so Anne was hoping this would be the beginning of something great.

In walks this man and woman, "Good afternoon" he said, "my name is Gordon, and this is my wife Lily", holding out his hand to Anne.

"Yes hello" said Anne "this is my husband Bert, nice to meet you both, have you got any experience in ballroom dancing?"

"Yes" he said, "we were indoor champions in 1952 in Glasgow, it was a tight contest, but we were the best couple", (*indoor? what the bloody hell* thought Anne, *there is no outdoor*).

"Ok" said Bert "sit over there and we'll sort out what we are doing when everyone turns up."

As Gordon walked over to the seat, Anne couldn't help but notice he was limping, ballroom dancing limping, funny old game this is.

"What's with the limp then?" Gordon asks Bert, pointing to Gordon's left leg, "how can you dance with a limp? Sorry mate but Anne and I only want the best, I say this with the greatest respect, but some of the routines are really testing and very upbeat."

"How dare you" said Gordon, "there's nothing my wife and I cannot do, if it comes to it, we are probably better than you, come on put a record on, come on I'll show you."

"Well, well ok" said Bert, "sorry Gordon but, but" Bert was in a right state, thinking *what the bloody hell did I say that for?*

"Right, oh let's all calm down, it's just that Anne and my self want the best dancers and the best dance group in the city."

"Yes, and we don't want to join one that hasn't got the drive and the best dancers in town" said Gordon, "so put on a record and we will show you."

"Ok" Anne said, "Bert lets see what Gordon and Lily have got."

Anne put on a quickstep, Gordon and Lily were just fine, in fact they were quite good, but Gordon's limp could be seen, when he turned, he seemed to be off balance. So, Gordon and Lily were 'signed on' so to speak. Bert said he could put them in the middle of the group, and no one would notice Gordon's limp.
Gordon said he was happy with that, but pointed out to Bert that he wanted to lead the group by the time they were ready to enter competitions, he wanted to be the lead.
"Yes ok" said Bert, not too sure if he's doing the right thing letting Gordon and Lily join the group. Anne thinks Bert's too fussy, and that Gordon will be just fine.

Gordon and Lily were well liked by the rest of the group, Gordon was soon the butt of some good, humoured banter, his nick name was jock strap, he didn't mind at all, he thought it was funny and knew it was just banter, he gave just as much back as he took, so it equalled itself out.
Jock strap was a tight bastard, he would never buy a round of drinks even if it was his turn, he would disappear into the toilets then show up after the round was in and say, "oh bloody hell who's brought that round it was my turn". He was that tight it was said he used to turn the grill off to turn his bacon over, yeah bloody too right.
He didn't like anyone calling round his house, collecting anything you know, salesmen, Jehovah's witnesses and so forth. He used to say, "fucking begging bastards, they only put the money in their own pockets."
One day someone knocked his door, "hello I'm collecting for Birmingham Brass Band would you like to donate something?"

"What?" he said holding his hand to his ear as if he was deaf.
"I'm collecting for the Birmingham Brass Band would you like to donate anything?"
"What?" Jock said, again holding his hand to his ear. "I'm collecting…" *oh fuck it* the guy thought and walked off down the path. Jock said, "shut the gate please!" the guy whispered to himself *fuck you*, Jock shouted, "fuck your Birmingham Brass Band as well, ha!" tight bastard.

Jockstraps limp was acquired in a traffic accident, he used to work for the D.V.L.A as a test inspector, one day he was testing a guy on a scooter, he said, "right, drive around the block and at some point on the main road I will jump out and hold my hand up, you will then jam on your brakes, its called an emergency stop, ok off you go, keep to the speed limit, be aware when you come up the main road."
Everything is set, Jock's standing there waiting for his scooter, he's done this hundreds of times, up comes this scooter out jumps Jock with his hand in the air, BANG the scooter crashes into Jockstrap. Bloody hell it was the wrong scooter. Jock's lying there out of it, leg broken, blood everywhere, *shit* he thinks *what am I doing?* He was rushed to hospital and had a small operation on his leg. Later, after he had recovered, he realised that he had a limp, he tried everything to get it right; physio, leg stretched, nothing worked. So, he was stuck with a slight limp (should have gone to Specsavers).

After a few weeks Bert and Anne had assembled quite a good group. There was a good mixture of young and old. Practice, practice, practice! was Bert's motto. He was never rude to anyone, always smiling and always ready with advice. Everybody looked forward to Mondays and Thursdays, week after week they got better and better, there were always new people wanting to join, which was good. It kept everyone on their toes, ballroom toes yes.

One Monday afternoon just as Bert was ready for rehearsals, in walked a Jamaican couple, everyone looked around. *Good god* Jockstrap thought *I hope they have just come to watch, they're too big to dance* (wrong again Jockstrap).
"Hello," said Anne, "how are you? can I be of any help?" smiling at them.
"Yes, we would like to join your dance club. We are both very interested in ballroom dancing."
"Well yes" said Anne "sit down and we'll have a chat," at that Bert put a record on and everyone started to dance.
Anne sat down with the couple, "right" she said, "I'm Anne, and that's my husband Bert", pointing to Bert as he was putting everyone through their paces.
"I'm Matilda, and this is my husband Rupert, but just call me Tilly" she said, "and do you mind if I smoke?"
"Yes, that's fine" said Anne (you could smoke in most places then). Tilly then pulled a big pipe out of her handbag and lit it up. Bloody hell it was like a chimney stack, clouds of smoke everywhere, Anne was waving her hand about trying to clear the smoke away.
"Sorry" said Tilly.
"No, no" Anne said still trying to see Tilly through the smoke, "but what's in it?"
"Oh, just some black shag, it's a nice smoke," said Tilly. By this time all the dance troupe were coughing and missing their steps.

"Stop, stop!" shouts Bert "what's all this smoke?" waving his hands around.
"Oh, its Till's pipe," said Anne.
"Yes, ok" said Bert "but not while we're dancing."

"Right let's have a cup of tea, shall we?" says Bert. They all sat down around the tables at the end of the dance floor, Tilly says she would like to show Anne a few dance steps to see if she and Rupert were good enough to join the dance troupe.
"Ok what dance would you like to do then?" asks Anne smiling.
"The waltz, Foxtrot whatever" says Tilly.
"Right Foxtrot then, are you ready?" Anne puts on a record and the rest of the group sit there with their tea and watch. Jockstrap says, "this should be good" looking at everybody, "I don't think". But how wrong he was. As the music starts, Tilly and Rupert square up and away they go. For two people who are about 15 stone each, well Rupert was 18 stone, they were good. No, *really* bloody good. So sleek, so precise were their steps, they glided across the floor like two pro's. Jockstrap was gobsmacked and so were the rest of the group.
Anne and Bert looked at each other, "what have we here?" they both said together. Tilly and Rupert finished their dance and walked over to the rest of them. Everyone clapped them.
"Thank you" said Tilly, "were we ok then?"
"Yes, yes" said Anne "where did you learn to dance like that?"
"We worked for an English man who had this big house in Jamaica and every week he and his wife had ballroom dancing and all the staff were allowed to go and the master taught us to dance quite well don't you think?"

"He certainly did" says Bert, "and welcome to our dance club", then he went through the days and times they met, also Wednesday night was all ballroom, so two more to add to the dance troupe.

The next few weeks were all full of fun, just learning new dances and everyone was getting on just fine, all except Jockstrap. He still wanted to be the lead and kept on bitching about it. "Listen Jock" said Bert, "It's ok when we are dancing with partners around the dance floor, but when we have to do the line dancing, like the military two step, you can't go up front because of your limp! how many more times jock?"
"So, if I hadn't got a limp, I'd be ok to head the group?" said Jock.
"Well, yes Jock of course you would" says Bert, "but you have, and you can't. So just shut up please."
Jockstrap was a bloody pain, but he was determined to lead the team one way or another. He had a mate who worked in a cobblers and had a chat with him one day in the pub, "listen, my best mate" he said, "I've had this idea of how to get rid of my limp, and I need your help ok".
"Yes of course" said his mate, "but how on earth can I help you get rid of your limp? Break your other leg ha, ha?"
"No, you prat just shut up and listen, right, can you sort out my shoes, sort of build one of them up so to level my leg to the same length as the other? but not a fucking club foot, ok? I want to be able to dance without a limp, yes or no, can you do it?" Ted Tanner the cobbler (yes, yes, I know) said he would try, so the next day Jockstrap went into Ted's shop to get measured up for his new shoes.

A few days later Jockstrap tried on the shoes and after a few minor alterations, things were looking good. Jockstrap also got some new trousers, a bit longer than his others so when he put them on you couldn't see his shoes. He and his wife tried them out at the local club, and they were bloody brilliant, you couldn't tell he had a limp at all.
"Right then" he said to his wife, "let's not tell anyone shall we?"
"Of course not" she said smiling.

Monday afternoon, into the Queens walks Jockstrap and his wife, "hi everybody" he said all smiles.
"Hello to you!" everyone shouted.
"He's in a good mood" says Bert.
"Let's not spoil it" says Anne, "keep quiet Bert."
"Before we start" says Jockstrap, "can I just show you something Bert?" sticking his chest out. *What now* thinks Bert.
"Put the Military Two Step on please Anne," said Jock.
"Yes ok" she said raising her eyebrows and looking at Bert as if to say *why us?*
"Ok my dear" says Jockstrap to his wife, "lets show them", and off they go, one two, one two, in, out, in, out and not a limp in sight.
"God, what's the bloody form?" says Anne to Bert, "what's happened to his limp? he looks good, doesn't he?"
"Well yes" says Bert "but, oh god I don't know what to say, turn it off Anne please. Just turn it off and let's see what Jocks got to say about it."
"Well, what do you think then Bert?" asks Jock.
"Yes", said Bert "but where's the limp gone?"

"Does it really matter?" Bert says Jock, "It's gone so come on let me be the leader, come on Bert you said I could if I hadn't got a limp."
Bert was just stumped, "yes," he said, "you're right, but what's with the new leg then?"
"Does it really mater Bert? I'm ok and ready to lead, so any problem then mate, yes, or no?"
Bert looked at Anne "shall we then dear?" he asks.
"Ok, I'm happy" said Anne "how about the rest of the gang, do you want Jock to lead you?"
They all looked at each other, "yes ok" was the general answer, so Jockstrap was put up to the front of the troupe.

He and his wife were good dancers and even better now he'd got rid of his limp. There was a competition coming up in two weeks time, the British Legion also had a ballroom team and a good one at that, they had already won the Midlands Championship and had gotten through to the semi finals of the British Championships so it's a tall order for Bert, Anne, and the team.
This competition was the charity cup, only for clubs in and around Birmingham, it would be a good scalp if Bert and Anne could beat the British Legion.
They were drawn at the Queens which was good, home advantage and all that. It was held on a Wednesday night and the hall was full, the competition lasted one hour so there was plenty of time for everyone to enjoy dancing the rest of the night.
It was just manic, the atmosphere was electric, what a night this is going to be.

Bert and Anne were on the team, and they were always at the back when the line dances were performed, the Military Two step and so on, they would keep the strictest of eyes on the troupe and pass messages on up the line if need be. They were very capable dancers and very methodical and loved every minute of their time running the dance club. They could with their talent go a lot further, but they were both only interested in their dance team, it meant so much to them, it was like their little baby that they never had, so when the competition night arrived, they were like two kids ready to open their Christmas presents.

There were two rooms at the Queens that they used to change into their dance costumes, but not all dance clubs had two changing rooms, most just had a place in the corner with a screen around them and you had to just get on with it when changing, but most of the men had seen it all before and never bothered when they saw the girls in just knickers and bra (really?) but tonight there was a bit more privacy.
"Ok" Bert says, "let's get our dance heads on and let's do some stretching", all part of the build-up.
"We're on first" said Anne, "first off, a foxtrot then we have the Argentine Tango, Jockstrap keep your head back and your back straight".
"Yes ok" says Jock.
"Nancy and Paul make sure you look at each other with passion just like we practiced."
This was the theme of the night, wind everyone up and make sure they were up for the fight, "remember" said Bert "they have to beat us not us beat them, hearts beating, brows sweating let's go for it", out they go to a wonderful reception and by God did they do well, it was a very impressive performance by the Queens team. Very, very professional and the other team looked at each other as if to say we've got it all to do, a mountain to climb.

Bert and Anne were very proud of their team and there were a few tears in the dressing room. "Well bloody done" said Bert "I'm so proud of you all, the British Legion have got it all to do so let's go out there and watch them."
Out come the Legion team and well, they were just fantastic, what a bloody close competition this was, just one point in it.
The Legion won by one point; their team captain said the Queens team was the best they had seen for years. Anne said, "another day, another dance, come on we were not disgraced", and off they went to the bar to have a drink with the opposition.
All the judges were of the same opinion, the Queens were ready to be the next dance champions of the Midlands.

Monday afternoon everyone met up, most of the team were over sixty and had no problem turning up on the afternoons, the younger ones of the team were on shifts so had to work around their shifts.
"Ok" says Anne "let's get our act together and work on our faults", the judges said this, and the judges said that it's all analysed what went wrong last week.
Everyone was down, they thought they had done enough to win and when Bert says let's get practicing, they were not too enthusiastic, but like true pro's they got on with it.
"Right" says Anne, "teatime", they all sit down as they always did halfway through dance class and as always those who smoked lit up and had a good old puff.
Tilly said she needed to have some of her special tobacco, her husband said no not now.
"Oh, shut up" Tilly says, "I'm down so kiss my rass you bumber". The smoke from Tilly's pipe was more than

usual, the smell was more pungent, it soon spread through the group all sitting there drinking tea. Jockstrap said, "that's a nice smell".
"Do you think so?" says his wife.
"Yes", said Jockstrap.
Bert says, "is that new tobacco Tilly?"
"Yes, sort of" she says smiling at Bert. Then after a while one or two of the team start to cheer up, Nancy says "shall we have a jive?"
"Yes" said Noel "put on a rock record."
"Yes" said Jockstrap, "let's get rocking", soon everyone was in the same frame of mind and Jockstrap put on a rock song. Everyone got up and started to jive, they just let it all go, it was hilarious. There was some funny sights and some excellent dancing, everyone was really out of it, yes, all the team were rocking and rolling. Anne thought they had all gone mad and she walked off to the toilet, Bert just about got himself together and said, "ladies and gentlemen please, come on let's have some decorum, shall we? come on we're strictly ballroom not rock and roll."
No chance, everyone was just gone, Bert stood there shaking his head, "and what's that bloody smell?" he said, his head was spinning, and his eyes were running. Just then, Alphonse appeared at the top of the stairs, "well, well what's all this then Bert?" He said, "has everyone gone mad and what's all this smoke?"
"It's Tilly's pipe" said Bert "she likes a drag when we have our tea break".
"What's she got in it? I've smelt this before" said Alphonse, and he walks up to Tilly. "What the hell have you got in there?" he said.
"Oh, just my special weed" she said.
"Weed?" said Alphonse "I hope you don't mean cannabis?"

"No, no" said Tilly, "its Indian Hemp, and its cheered everyone up so no harm done."

"No harm done?" says Alphonse "it's bloody illegal! put the damn thing out for god sake before you get us all arrested and the place shut down!" then he takes the pipe off Tilly and puts it out. The record had just finished, and all the dance team were totally out of it. Bert was smiling, he was a bit lightheaded but pulled himself together. Anne was ok, she had gone to the toilet, so she was more than aware of what Alphonse was saying.

"Right" she said, "dance class has finished, everyone up to the restaurant for some coffee", they all trouped off upstairs gingerly.

Anne says to Alphonse, "we can't let them out of the dance hall yet, can we?"

"Oh, bloody hell" says Alphonse "what a game this is, I've got the dance floor to polish, and the bar to clean, I can't do that with all this lot here can I? the cleaners will be here in 30 minutes, and they won't be too pleased if this lots still here."

Anne's got an idea (good old Anne) she puts it past Alphonse, he's gobsmacked, "do you think they can?" he asks.

"Yes, I do" says Anne. "Right, you lot!" Anne shouts, "get yourselves together and line up on the dance floor".

"Ok, ok" everyone says, thinking they were going to do another dance, they all spread across the dance floor in a line, then Anne handed them all mops and polish, "right to your right, to your left, come on get your arms working", they all thought it very funny but it worked, they all started to sashay down the dance floor and soon they were singing and the dance floor never looked so clean.

After a while most of the troupe were back to normal, "thank God" says Anne. Bert was a bit embarrassed he had lost control of things, so he pulled himself and everyone together and gave them a good old bollocking, and Tilly? Well, she never smoked the pipe again, not in the dance hall anyway.

Over the next few years, the Queens dance troupe won some gongs and were well known as one of the best dance troupes around the Midlands. They met the British Legion quite a few times over the years and to date the Queens lead 4 to 1, well done everyone.
Bert and Anne were just fabulous, they were respected by everyone, they never missed a dance class, they used to have a break in the summer for a few weeks as the ballroom scene was quiet then (that's the competitions). Wednesday was still a good night (ballroom) whatever the time of year.
Anne had a history of Bronchitis, mostly in the winter, she was strong and coped with it, but as she got older, she found it harder to fight it. One winter was particularly cold and poor old Anne was really ill, she was rushed off to hospital one night as her breathing was very shallow, it then turned to pneumonia, she never recovered and poor old Anne died. Bert was devastated, she was his rock they had been inseparable, they had no children, there was just the two of them. Their life had just been ballroom and the people in and around the Queens.
Anne had a good send off, she was liked by everyone and was sadly missed.
Bert tried to get himself together but when you loved someone like Bert loved Anne you can't just say, "oh well onward and upward", he tried hard to cope with it, Jockstrap took over the dance club while Bert was in

mourning. Bert had so much support from everyone, but it was a struggle, no one knew what to say to Bert, sometimes he was ok, then sometimes someone would say something quite innocent, and Bert would fall back into depression, this went on for months.

Bert went off on his usual holiday to Margate, every year Bert and Anne would descend on Margate and do the same thing they had done for years, dance, dance some more and sit on the pier and sing their favourite song (bright and breezy free and easy) with their fish and chips. They loved it, every year the same thing, some people went to different places every year, been there, lets see something else, not Bert and Anne, Margate was their paradise, boy if it aint broke don't mend it.

Bert sat in the pier bar, he loved the pier, and he loved the dancing they had at the small club at the back of the bar, today Bert was drinking pint after pint with whiskey chasers. One after another, "you ok?" says the barman, he knew Bert and Anne very well, so he was concerned with Bert's heavy drinking, Bert only ever had three pints, never any more, so quite rightly the barman was worried about Bert. Also, in Bert's pocket was half a bottle of whiskey, every other pint he had a good swig from the bottle, then after a few drinks Bert went and sat in Anne and his favourite seat at the end of the pier looking out to sea, they would sit there and sing and hold hands, they were so much in love. Bert sat there with Anne's photo in his hand, he opened a bottle of pills (sleeping tablets) and downed the lot with the rest of the bottle of whiskey. Soon, Bert's eyes were heavy he was struggling to stay awake, one more slug of whiskey then the bottle fell to the floor, Bert had one more look at Anne's photo then looked up to the sky then out to sea, he started singing their favourite song very very slowly, bright and breezy free and easy, then Bert's head fell forwards. That's where a P.C. found him some time later… Bert was dead. He couldn't live without Anne, he left a note to say sorry to everyone, Bert had planed this a few weeks before he came to Margate, he had sorted his funeral and his house, it was a council house, and any cash left over was going to their favourite charity.

Everyone at the Queens were shocked, they never thought that Bert would do this, he also had a good send off and was buried with Anne, they had both gone to that big ballroom in the sky.

Jockstrap took over the dance team and he and his wife did a great job, at the bottom of the dancehall where the club sat when they had their tea break, was a big silver plaque on the wall that read: "To Anne and Bert, sadly missed, LEGENDS."

CHAPTER THREE

Saturday night rock and roll, one of the busiest nights of the week. Alphonse walked around the Queens as he did most nights making sure everything and everyone was ok. Saturday was special, it was the weekend and most of the punters just wanted a good time, dance, drink, and eat. I say most, there were a few who would just sit at the bar and chill out, they didn't want anything too energetic, so Alphonse would take extreme care that things went as smoothly as possible.
"Bar ok Steve?" Alphonse would say, "all staff ready for the onslaught?"
"Yes boss" Steve would reply.
"Steve, how many more times do I have to tell you, its Alphonse?"
"Ok boss… sorry, Alphonse ha."
Steve would give Alphonse the V sign, behind his back that is.

"Restaurant ok Pam?" He asks.
"Just fine Alphonse, thank you" she replied, "would you like a cup of tea?"
"No thanks" Alphonse would say, "I don't like tea."
Pam knew this, that's why she would ask him, get rid of him as quickly as possible, she was too busy to stand chatting to Alphonse.
Then he would walk around the dance floor chatting to everyone asking, "are you enjoying yourselves?"
"Everything ok?" "What do you think of the entertainment?" Generally being polite to everyone. However, not all punters were polite back, after a few pints at the bar you got your run of the mill idiots, no fighting just gobby, "hey Alfy how long you had that

wig?" "You want to get some good entertainment on you wanker."
"And what's that then lads?" Alphonse would say, "strippers?"
"Yeah" they would reply, "let's see some tits ha!"
"That's enough of that you lot, anymore and you're out" says Alphonse, and the lads would run off laughing then. Alphonse would laugh to himself, *cheeky bastards.*

Then on to the stage, make sure everything was ready to roll, rock as well. With all this done he would go to his office and have a stiff drink, look in the mirror, straighten his tie, then out to the front of the Queens to check how much cash they were taking. Alphonse would then go back to his office, have another stiff drink, then ring head office and tell them things were ok. Mecca had this discipline with all their dance halls, keep their finger on the pulse as they would say.
Alphonse was standing by the main bar when a young couple asked if they could have a word. "Yes sure" said Alphonse, "what can I do for you?" The girl said, "you know Cliff Richard?"
"Yes" said Alphonse.
"Well can you get him to sing here?"
"Get him to sing here?" said Alphonse.
"Well yes why not? he's the one who thinks he's Elvis yeah?"
"No" said the lad, "he's our Elvis, he's good, any chance then?"
"Yes" says Alphonse, "a phone call in the right place and you never know", touching his nose, "leave it with me I'll get back to you."
(he's got more chance of finding a rocking horse shit in his office than getting Cliff to sing at the Queens, he's just gone global) Alphonse would try, he couldn't do

enough for his punters, and can you believe it, Cliff was booked solid for the next 12 months. Well, who wants Cliff Richard when we can have Quasimodo, the best band in the world? Quasi always answers the call from Birmingham and never disappointed his fans.

"Yes, I've spoken to Cliff's agent" said Alphonse next time he saw the couple, "he's very busy at the moment but will get back to us as soon as he's free" (as if) and off he goes into the restaurant.
Pam was up to her neck in the kitchen, she was helping Jeff who was losing it tonight, he had a few problems with the ovens and to say he was under pressure was an understatement.
"Where's Pam?" was Alphonse's first words as he walks into the restaurant, "helping in the kitchen" said Stella, "we've got problems with the ovens, and as you can see, we are not exactly quiet, are we?" Stella was trying to serve and take orders at the same time.
"Right" said Alphonse, and off he strides into the kitchen, "ok Pam, off you go" he says, "I'll help out in here, go on, its not a problem for me", and he's soon helping Jeff and his staff. Jeff's not too sure that Alphonse can perform as well as talks.
"Ok Alphonse" said Jeff, "put those spuds in the chip pan, and cut that chili into pieces, get that tart out of the fridge…" and on and on he went. *Bloody hell* Alphonse thought, *I've opened my big mouth again.*
"Come on lads" said Jeff "chop, chop."
"Ok chef!" was the reply.

Jeff was doing a flambé with flames coming off the pan. Alphonse looked up, *Christ* he thought *there's a fire!* and grabbed the fire extinguisher and put it out.

"You bloody idiot!" shouted Jeff, "what the hell are you doing? You've worked in enough hotels to know what a flambé is!"
"Sorry, sorry!" said Alphonse, "I got carried away."
"Well please just leave us" said Jeff, "and go and run the dance competition."
"Ok" said Alphonse throwing his head back in disgust.

Steve was looking at this bird who was standing by the bar, she was by herself having a quiet drink, *mm* thinks Steve *she's a bit of alright*. Steve was a womaniser, Pam would catch him out one day but until then, Steve played the field. This girl looked to be about 20-25 years old, nice long hair, very slender, not too much makeup. Steve made sure Pam wasn't in the vicinity, then he again made sure the bird was on her own. Yep, looks like it, so Steve moves in for the kill, "well hello sweetie and how's things with you? Enjoying yourself? I haven't seen you here before, would you like to have a drink with me? I'm the bar manager, then perhaps we can go onto some where later yes? No?" This girl looks Steve in the eye and says, "I'll say this just once, I am P.C. Holloway on surveillance, so get yourself back behind your bar and help your staff to serve all your customers waiting for a drink, and by the way, I know Pam quite well, so just fuck off."
Steve never moved so quick in his life, *shit* he thinks *what's all that about, fuck me I hope she doesn't tell Pam, shit* (what goes around comes around, that's what they say).
Down on the dance floor, things were crazy, it was every Saturday, but tonight was dance competition night. Twenty couples start then three judges walk around and touch one couple on the shoulder, then they must leave the dance floor and so on until there are three

couples left. Then there's a break for the band to come on for an hour and then the dance off.
Tonight, Nigel Parker, known as 'nosy', and his mate Dave Langston, known as 'laugher', as he was always laughing throughout the competition. They both were good at jiving, all the girls wanted to dance with them. Tonight, dancing with the lads were two charmers, Doreen 'drop um' Reynolds, and 'just put the end in' Edna (if you'll excuse the expression) they all had nicknames then, they were also good dancers, so the dance off should be good.

"Ladies and gentlemen, the dance off!" announces the compare, "let's hear it for the finalists, come on!" the crowd respond and cheer, clap, and stamp the floor. He introduces the three couples and off they go, each couple chooses a song they like so its fair for all, they all dance to the three songs and the judges pick 1st 2nd and 3rd. It's hot, it's noisy, and it's bloody great. The atmosphere, well all one can say is its electric, these dance competitions were the highlight of the night, they were held most Saturdays.

You also saw some funny sights on the dance floor, Jake and Frankie were a good laugh, Jake used to throw Frankie over his shoulder and then through his legs. Then stand her on the top of his bended legs, but sometimes, just for a giggle, Jake used to let Frankie go when she went through his legs, she would slide into the crowd then the crowd would push her back to Jake, all in good fun.
Alice used to love showing her knickers, all the lads used to shout "show us your knickers Alice! come on do the splits!" she was good, but a show off, she always danced with Dave, he was gay, but for a gay bloke he

pulled some birds! One night, Alice was dancing with Dave in the Saturday dance off when she did the splits, but her knickers ripped in half and dropped to the floor, what a bloody sight, everybody was shouting and cheering. Poor Alice, she was so embarrassed, but Dave came to the rescue, he picked up her torn knickers and led her off the dance floor and to the ladies toilets (yes, I said the ladies toilets not the lads).

Nosy and his partner won tonight, they were the best on the night, depending on how much booze he had on the night he was probably the best male dancer in the hall (rock and roll).
Nosy was a window cleaner by day, (as I've said, he got his nick name from his surname being Parker) he was once caught in one of his lady customers bedroom, she was lying on the bed and he was just taking his trousers off when in walked her husband, Nosy dived out the window and fell down the ladder. The husband threw the bucket of soapy water all over Nosy, he was certainly a 'jack the lad', but that day he was a wet and bruised jack the lad.

There were so many different characters in the Queens, never a dull moment, whatever night it was.
Saturday was so loud and so hot, but everyone loved every minute of it. Dance competition over, the bands on playing loud rock numbers, so many people on the dance floor, some just carried away with the music, some just talking to each other, some girls dancing with each other, also some lads, nobody bothered in the sixties, you just let yourself go.
In the restaurant were Susan and John Thomas, they never missed a Saturday night at the Queens, tonight they decided to not dance and just to watch. Sue was

eight and a half months pregnant, so she thought it best not to dance tonight, they both watched the dance competition and were shouting and jumping up and down in the restaurant when suddenly, Sue's water broke, and she went into labour. It was so quick, John lowered Sue to the floor and said "please, someone ring an ambulance! My wife's having a baby!" Pam came running over to help and made sure Sue was as comfortable as possible, they all stood around Sue, "give her some air!" shouts Pam. Alphonse came running in, "I've rang an ambulance its on its way", Sue was screaming, "it's coming out!"

"Oh god, ok, ok" said Pam "just push, come on push!"
"Push?" Shouts Alphonse, "in here? the bloody restaurant? You can't do that, tell her to hang on."
"Oh, shut up Alphonse" said Pam "it's half way out!" Everyone on the dance floor stopped dancing, the band stopped playing, everyone was looking up to the restaurant, and all were shouting *push come on push!* With all this encouragement, Sue pushed and pushed. "There's the head!" shouted John, and soon out popped the wee one right as ninepence, with one big cry and air in the baby's lungs everything was ok.

The dance hall was again the focus of a drama, soon the band started playing again and everyone was dancing and having fun, the ambulance took Sue and the baby away (it was a girl) they stayed in hospital for a few days, then off home to John. Sue and John called the baby Elizabeth, they had already decided on a name before the birth, if it had been a boy, it would have been Peter. Anyway, two weeks later Sue and John went to the Queens to see Alphonse and Pam to thank them for their help, and would they mind if they called baby Elizabeth, Queen Elizabeth after the dance hall.

"Yes" said Alphonse "we will have a photo of you and Liz put up in the foyer", which they did and under the photo was the inscription *"Queen Elizabeth was born here on Saturday 9th June 1964".*

It made some good media news, also it was on the TV and the baby and parents throughout there lives made a few quid.

Alphonse and Pam were also rewarded by Mecca, the Queens dance hall was the talk of the Midlands for years to come. Queen Elizabeth born there, no kidding.

CHAPTER FOUR

Terry Cooper was a really good-looking bloke, 6ft 2in, jet black hair (dyed), pencil moustache, he looked like Clark Gable, the heart throb film star, and didn't he know it. He was the regular compare at the Queens, a real charmer, all the ladies loved him, they would all love to shag him, (that's what they tell each other). He would play them up every night, some of the young rockers thought he was a wanker, they would say "I bet he's a poof", (they weren't far wrong). Terry was AC/DC, if you know what I mean. He loved young men as well as young ladies, a few old ones as well, but Terry's job was to charm the ladies, he would eyeball a different one each night, you know, pick one out and make sure he paid her plenty of attention, it always worked.

The management gave him a bonus if he could get more women around the stage, Alphonse used to say, "Terry, we need your charm and charisma to make sure all these ladies come back, so do your damn best." He certainly did, night after night, he'd pick on one woman and say, "you're so beautiful, have you got a monopoly on beauty? God why are you on your own? You know with the right guidance you could be a top model." (even to the ugly ones), "I'm not just saying this to shag you darling, I really mean it, listen kid I've been in show business for some time and I know what I'm talking about!" It usually worked, two gin and tonics and all the patter, yes Terry was the ladies favourite.

Mondays and Tuesdays were more or less the same, Mondays dancing, foxtrot, waltz, tango, and rock. But Tuesdays were slightly different, they had a free and easy, punters getting on the stage to sing, some good, mostly bad, but for all it was fun, everybody loved the band (they were a 12-piece band) they knew how to wind up the crowd. "Ok" Terry would say, "what are you going to sing?" Then the girl or guy would say whatever song they wanted, then the band would play it loud and fast for about twenty seconds, "ok then, are you ready to go, yes, no?" Everyone on the dance floor would come down to the stage and start cheering and there would be plenty of encouragement. "Come on, let's hear it for so and so", it was so spontaneous, it was all fun no one took it seriously, but it made the night (no karaoke machines then my friends) you had to hope you could remember the words and just go for it, it was all new to the punters and didn't they just love it.

Monday night 7:30 doors open, plenty of punters, queues were down the street, it was two bob to get in the Queens on a Monday, it was a popular night so two bob was money well spent.
There used to be guys standing outside the Queens who had no money, they had spent out over the weekend, but it was such a good gig everyone wanted to be there. "Lend us two bob Frank, I'll give it you back Friday." or "open the side door John, will you?" They all wanted to get into the Queens,
Alphonse had flashing red lights over all the fire exits, so if one was opened the red light would flash and the door staff would race over to catch whoever the perpetrator was. Sometimes they would be shoved back outside, probably to try again later, sometimes the guy or girl trying to get in through these exits would say, "hold on mate I just feel sick that's all, and I need to go out for some fresh air" (oh yeah) sometimes it worked,

most times it didn't. The Queens was such a hot place to be that punters would do almost anything to get in. Terry stood by the side of the stage watching all the women strut their stuff, fat ones, thin ones, tall ones, small ones, posh ones, common as muck ones, drunk ones, and gobby ones, but dance night at the Queens, nobody gave a shit, they're all in it together, all having fun.
Some of the girls were in groups all dancing round their handbags (there were nights when purses were nicked out of the bags if left on their seats) some dancing in two's, eyeing up the guys standing at the side, (not many guys dancing in twos to a waltz or foxtrot) every night was magic always something going on.

Tonight, Terry was playing up to this posh bird, he had tried to pull her last week, but she got too drunk and went home with her friends. He was making eyes at her just as the band were about to finish their number, "announce the next dance please" said the band leader, Terry quickly walked to the mic and said, "who knows how to do the Bossa Nova?" Knowing the posh bird was good at this dance as he'd seen her doing it last week. Then looking right at this bird, "yeah you do" he says, she hasn't said anything yet, this is Terry's way of pulling a bird. Some think its great and play up to him, some, like this bird, think *you can just fuck off you're not embarrassing me,* Terry again looking at her, repeats his request, "Bosso Nova? Yes, come on don't be shy, I'll dance with you."
Terry was quite a good dancer, and most women would jump at the request, but no, this one was having none of it. She starts to walk off the dance floor, Terry prompts the band leader to play the Bossa Nova then jumps off the stage and grabs this woman by the arm, "don't be a

spoil sport, let's just dance!" and he starts to dance, "come on let's swing baby", she responds, and they make a good pair, everyone as always was clapping. Terry starts his chat up line, "I've seen you here most weeks."
"Ten out of ten for observation." the girl says. *This could be hard work* thinks Terry.
"You're such a good dancer" said Terry, "are you professional? no? would you like to teach me then?"
"No", she says.
"Well, would you like me to teach you how to say yes?" he said smiling at her. She then starts smiling herself, "oh you're such a bloody charmer, aren't you?" she says. *At fucking last* thinks Terry, and they end up having a good laugh.

Terry then gets back to his job as compare, she dances with him again, then there's a break and off they go to the bar for a drink.
"What's your name then?" asks Terry.
"I was wondering when you were going to ask" she said, "it's Penny, Penny Armstrong."
"Nice name" says Terry, "there's a car sales pitch in town called Armstrong's, the boss is a right con man."
"Is he?" said Penny, "I'll tell him later, he's my dad."
"Oh. err yes, I am only joking" said Terry, "he's a nice man ha." *Oh, fuck me here we go* thinks Terry.
"Oh, don't bullshit" says Penny, "does he know you then?"
"Well sort of" says Terry, "I know him through a friend, never dealt with him myself but you hear rumours, don't you?"
"Yes, you do, and yes, my dad is 'one of the lads' if you know what I mean, anyway never mind him, what are you doing later?" She asks.

"Me?" says Terry.
"Well, you I hope" she said laughing out loud.
"Why? have you got something or somewhere in mind?" said Terry.
"Yes," she said, "how about going to the Diamond club in the Bullring?"
"Yes ok" said Terry, *this is going to be easier than I thought* he thinks. So, Terry has pulled again and says see you later and off he goes back on stage smiling and eying all the birds up as he does so well.

Penny danced with him again and arranged to meet him outside when he had finished, she sat with her friends and watched Terry going through his paces, dancing with other girls, and playing to the crowd.
Penny's mates told her she's mad going with him, "look at him he's just a bloody perv! He'll get what he wants from you then it will be 'NEXT!' and you won't get a second look!"
"Ok" says Penny, "just watch this space."
The night is still young and the restaurant is in full swing, Pam's running around as usual, but she's happy in her job, she likes meeting people, she gets chatted up sometimes but just laughs it off, "not tonight darling" she would say, "got a husband to shag ok." Mind you, some nights she wished she hadn't (got a husband that is) as we know Steve's always trying to pull some bird and thinks he's bullet proof. So, Pam gets a bit tearful some nights, she says if I catch him that's the end, but she hopes all the rumours are not true.
Steve's still at it with the tills, nicking a pound here and a pound there, the bar staff are not entirely stupid, they know someone is taking cash out of the tills, and yes, they all think it is Steve, but catching him, well that's something they must try to do. Clark's the one who

watches Steve more than anyone, there would be nothing that Clark would have liked better than to catch Steve as he hated him. Clark had on many occasions spoken to Alphonse about this, mostly when Steve had been bullying the staff about the tills not tallying up at night. As already stated, it is only £10 -£15 a week but it was on a regular basis, the accountants were starting to question Alphonse on this, so it'd become an issue.

Clark says "please give me a chance to catch him" to Alphonse. "Well, apart from standing there all night watching him what can we do?" Says Alphonse.
"I've got this plan if you'll let me put it into action," said Clark.
"Go on, shoot let's hear it" says Alphonse.
"Right, we all know that there's cash missing most nights, don't we?" Says Clark, "so for a start, give Steve a week holiday and let's see if the tills cash up then."
"Well, that's no fucking good," says Alphonse, "all the staff will think 'oh this is a set up' and nobody will go near the tills if you know what I mean."
"No, no," says Clark, "I won't say anything to the staff about us checking the tills, just give Steve a week off and say fuck all to the staff about the tills, then if there's any cash missing then well, we will know someone else is at it wont we? That's the first step, the next step, I will tell you after Steve's holiday, so what do you think yes, or no?"
"Ok" says Alphonse, "But, how am I going to convince Steve to have a week off?"
"Easy," says Clark, "Steve's been a bit stressed lately, hasn't he? So just say 'Steve, have a break, you look bloody awful.'"
This was agreed, and they both said not to say anything to Pam.

Back to the dance floor and things were getting hot, the drinks had gone to some of the punter's heads, and some were just out of it. They were trying to dance but just laughing and falling around, nobody gave a shit.
Terry was ready to announce the winner of the raffle, tonight's prize was a free ticket to a gala night in two weeks' time, a well sought after prize, as these nights were special, so the raffle sold out quite quickly, it was sixpence a ticket (do you remember the tanner? It was actually worth something then, you could get a coffee or a glass of pop in the pub, a paper or half a pint of beer, it was one and a penny a pint, oh the good old days, yes, we all loved them, coming out not worried about what people said all that freedom).

"Ok," Terry says into the mic, "let's have a nice young lady to draw the winning ticket, let's see… how about you?" then pointing to this good-looking girl. She was gorgeous. Terry as usual had been scanning the dance floor for talent, he spots her, right then he thinks to himself, I'll ask if she's got a ticket and if so BINGO, get her on stage and palm her ticket, this trick was used in many working men's clubs at this time. What you do is, get whoever you want to win, get their ticket off them, keep it in your hand, then ask the person you called up to draw a ticket out of the drum or hat, they would then give you the ticket and you would change it for the one in your palm, thus the term "palming" and then read out the number, yes there were some bloody scams about in the sixties.
"Have you had a go on the raffle my dear?" Asks Terry.
"Yes, I have" she replied.
"Good," he said, "good lets have you up here chick, come on bring your ticket with you." She climbs onto the stage, long legs short skirt, all the lads cheering and

trying to look if they can see her knickers as she climbs onto the stage (bloody pervs). "Give me your ticket my love, right thank you, I'll just put that in my pocket for safety," which he pretends to do, "ok, lets have one of the lads on stage shall we." calls Terry, he ain't daft, he knows if the girl draws her own ticket there will be a riot. "You stand there chick, so you can draw the second ticket."

What Alphonse thinks as he's standing at the back of the bar area, *there's only one ticket, what's that bastard up to?*

Terry starts to turn the handle on the drum that the tickets are in, "ok son," he says to the lad, "turn around, no looking!" then the lad puts his hand in, "just get one ticket," said Terry, "have you got one?" Terry takes it off the lad without him seeing it. "Ok just stand there." Terry says, "and who are you with tonight son?"

"Oh, my mates" the lad replies.

"Come on, point them out to me then." said Terry, the lad puts his hand up to his eyes as the arc lights are very bright, "oh, there they are" he said.

"Where?" Says Terry, all this is to distract everybody's attention, while all this is going on Terry puts the drawn ticket in his pocket, then the girls ticket in his hand.

"Give your mate a cheer then lads!" and waves to them, "ok let's see what the ticket number is" and gives the lad the palmed ticket (I hope you're all following this) "ok, lets have some quiet then shall we, and what's your name son?" he asks the lad.

"Paul" the lad replies.

"Ok Paul, read out the number."

"74 red" says the lad.

"Who's got 74 red then?" shouts Terry, "come on, who's the winner?" No ones got the ticket, "oh, I forgot yours my dear" says Terry, looking all innocent, "let's see now," then puts his hand in his pocket and gives Paul the ticket, "read it out then Paul" handing him the mic.

"74 red," said Paul.

"Oh my god, I don't believe it, it's yours!" Terry said to the girl and gives her a hug. Then he gets the ticket off the lad, "just check that," he said to the band leader, "yes 74 red, well lets do the next one Paul." He puts his hand in pulls out another ticket and gives it to Terry and he reads the number out, 231 green. "Over here!" shouts a lad in the audience, so in fact the first ticket was the second. The girl and the lad were given a pass for the gala night, and the second one that Paul drew was then found on the floor by Terry who said, "oh one fell out, ok who's got this? number 15 red?"

"Me" says this girl.

"Ok, sorry no more gala tickets, but a nice bottle of wine awaits you at the bar" (phew all this just to get the bird.) Terry then takes the bird to the side of the stage and says, "well, who's a clever boy then? I got you the winning ticket, didn't I? so how about a date then yeah?" looking her up and down, "come on I put myself up front so you could win."

"Well, I don't know what you mean" she said, "but I can't have a date with you."

"And why not chick?" asks Terry.

"Well, my husbands over there waving to us and he would blow his top." This guy stood up and waved to Terry, fuck me he was so big 6ft 5ins, 18 stone of pure muscle.

"Christ he's bloody big," says Terry.

"Yes," she said, "he's the British heavyweight boxing champion, Birmingham's own left hook Harry leave um dead Davis."

"Oh ok," Terry's shaking in his boots.

"Shall I bring him over?" says the girl.
"No, no," says Terry, "just enjoy the gala night" and pushes her away and walks back on stage, *that was close* he thinks *got to watch my face, can't get it smacked in, can I?* (Not just yet).

Alphonse ripped into Terry, "what the bloody hells your game then? As if I didn't know, you can pay for the second gala ticket and the fucking wine, one day, one day…" Alphonse was shaking with fury, "you'll get yours!" they both stood looking at each other. "Your job is to gee the ladies up, not fuck every one of them!"
"Oh, come on Alphonse," Terry says, "give me ten out of ten for trying." then turned away and walked off. Alphonse didn't know Terry had palmed the raffle ticket; *good job* thinks Terry, what the eye don't see the heart don't grieve over.

There's a guy at the kiosk, thinks he's Elvis (think about it) "can I come in and sing a few songs?" he asks.
"Yes," says the door man, "two bob and in you go."
"Well, I actually haven't got two bob at the moment, but I sing really good" he said.
"Oh, do you?" replied the door man, "well no money, no entry, ok Elvis?"
"Mock thee not," says Elvis, "you are looking at the best look alike in the Bullring."
"Listen 'Elvis', or whatever your name is," said the door man, "two bob or just fuck off, understand?" Just then, Alphonse appears, "what's all this then?" he asks,
"Oh," says the doorman, "this guy wants to sing a few Elvis songs on stage, he says he's the best Elvis look alike in the UK, but he wants to come in for nothing."
"Oh, does he?" says Alphonse looking him up and down, "mm, he does look like Elvis, I wonder if he can

sing like him. Give us a tune then." says Alphonse, "if its good, you can come in and sing on the stage, if not, PISS OFF."

The guy then bursts into song right there on the front steps of the Queens, and by God he was good. Alphonse was impressed, "let him in John."

"Ok boss," said the doorman.

Alphonse then took Elvis down to the stage, "ok kid, just wait there and I'll see what we can do."

"This kid by the side of the stage thinks he's Elvis," Alphonse says to Terry, "have a word with the band then get him on, he's pretty good, I've heard him."

"Ok," says Terry.

"Ladies and gentlemen, at great expense, we have the best Elvis impersonator in the UK, lets hear it for him!" On this guy comes, real mean looking, long sideburns, jet black hair, lip curled up. The crowd just stood there deathly silent. "Come on then!" this one guy shouted, "get on with it." Then the band started playing Teddy Bear, suddenly Elvis comes to life, hips swinging, legs shaking, he starts to sing "Oh baby let me be your loving teddy bear" he was pretty good, a bit nervous to begin with but soon got it all together. The dance floor soon came to life, most of the lads trying to dance like Elvis, the girls just swaying and trying not to laugh at the lads. Teddy bear finished, the crowd cheered and clapped for him, Terry asks, "do you want another one?"

"Yes!" was the overall response, so Elvis sang two more numbers, then his voice started to go all croaky.

Terry thanks him and off he goes to the side of the stage where Alphonse was waiting for him, "You were ok kid," he said.

"Thanks," Elvis says, "can I sing every week? You know, just two or three songs? Well, to be honest, I only

know them three songs and my voice goes all to pot then."
"Well, learn some bloody more then!" says Alphonse, "anyway, we will have to have a chat with the band and see what they think, so see me later in my office and we'll see what we can come up with."
"Yeah, ok." says Elvis, "what time?"
"Half an hour" says Alphonse.
"Ok, yes fine" says Elvis all excited, "half an hour then."

Alphonse has already got a plan in mind, he just needs to talk to Terry and the band leader, "how about this kid singing every week? but get someone out of the audience to see if they are better than him, you know, every week have this spot 'take on Elvis' or something like that, we'll get it advertised then have an half hour spot, come on it will be fun, something different, get a couple of judges on stage. This kid is quite good, so he will be hard to beat, we'll get more punters in, well what do you think?"
Terry says "ok, but is there anything to be won?"
"Not really," says Alphonse, "unless we give them a free ticket for the next weeks dance."
It was agreed, Alphonse met the kid in his office and told him the plan, and the lad was over the moon, "can I practice in the daytime here?" he asked.
"In the daytime?" said Alphonse, "ain't you working then?"
"No, not at the moment," replied the lad, "I worked on the dustbins but had the sack for spending too much time singing and not emptying the bins."
"Well, as it happens," said Alphonse, "we are looking for another cleaner, moneys not good, but if you can do it the jobs yours."

The kid took the job, he just wanted to be near the music scene, well you won't get any better place than the Queens.

Every week the Elvis contest was a big hit, two or three guys would try their luck, but the kid was good and won quite easily. He was well liked by the staff, but God did he do your head in with all his body shaking when he was sweeping the floor. The brush was the mic, and it was two sweeps then "since my baby left me ha" then another two sweeps "I've found a new place to dwell" in the end everyone was singing Elvis songs all day.
After a few weeks the kid said he was going to try and get a job at Butlins, they were advertising for staff for the summer season, Alphonse had got contacts at Butlins and managed to pull a few strings, the kid got the job, and went on to be an Elvis impersonator at Butlins for a few years.
Alphonse was pleased for different reasons, because whenever he spoke to some of the staff, they would do an Elvis pose or say, "yes baby", or "yes, I dig that man". Yeah, who would want show business.

The night nearly over, it had again been hectic for all the staff. After the dance hall had emptied, they checked all the doors were locked and made sure no one was left in the toilets pissed up, then it's a drink at the bar for any staff that wants one, a bit of a chat then off home they all went. Alphonse and the head doorman locked up, put all the alarms on and looked forward to the next soiree.

Terry meets his posh bird Penny outside and off they go night clubbing. They were in the Diamond Club, it was full and noisy, Penny found a seat while Terry got the drinks. "Oh, this is cosy," says Terry.

"Yes." Penny agrees, then suddenly, she says to Terry, "you've been here before, haven't you?"
"Yes, some time ago, I can't quite remember when. Anyway, let's talk about you." says Terry.
She downs her drink in one and shouts the waiter over for another one, "come on, drink up." she says to Terry.
"Slow down chick," he replies.
"What's the matter, can't stand the pace then?" says Penny.
"Well, if that's the case," says Terry, "bring it on, let's get pissed!" and they both laughed.
Drink after drink Terry was amazed how this bird could put away so much booze, well not quite, she was actually tipping her drinks into a flowerpot by the side of the table, she wanted to stay sober. Not so Terry could shag her when pissed, which Terry thought he was going to do, no, she wanted to be sober so she can sort Terry out.
The last time Terry was in the club was with Penny's brother, he was only eighteen, and I've said before, Terry was AC/DC and wanted to pull the boy for some fun, the boy got pissed and fell down the stairs to the toilet and broke his arm. Terry left him there, and the bouncers found him sitting there crying, Terry had done a runner, the wanker. The boy's dad said he would find Terry and sort him out, so this is what Penny was up to, revenge.
Sitting over the other side of the club was Ted Armstrong, and two heavies, just waiting for the right time to sort out Terry, (what goes around comes around).
Terry was out of it by now, he was trying to kiss Penny, she was playing up to him, "right, shall we go to my place then?" she asks kissing him on the cheek.
"Yeah, ok come on, let's get a taxi." says Terry.

"I think you should go to the toilet first and freshen up a bit, don't you think?" says Penny. As Terry walked unsteadily to the toilet, Penny waved to her dad.
Terry was found in the toilets by the bouncers, he was in a right mess, two black eyes, his mouth all swollen, he'd had a right old battering. No comparing for Terry for a couple of weeks, but what happens outside of the Queens, stays there.

CHAPTER FIVE

Thursday lunch time Steve's checking the bar and filling up the shelves, Clark was helping him and kept telling Steve how ill he looked, "do I?" says Steve, "well, I don't feel ill, so get on with your job." Lunch times were fairly busy, but no alcohol, just soft drinks from the small bar. There were always plenty of girls in at lunch time, it was the 'in thing', "let's have lunch at the Queens, a few dances to the records, then back to work." This period of the sixties was great, dance halls open at dinner time, never been known before, but it was well liked and full most lunch times.

Clark was trying to set the scene so that Alphonse could get Steve to have a week's holiday, but he was having no luck at all. Alphonse says he will have a word with head office and try some other way to get Steve out for a few days.
Thursday night was just records with Vince and Sally, it was another good night, mostly young bloods, never any trouble just plenty of fun. Sally would dance on the stage to some of the records, she was great fun, all the lads would try and date her, but she would have none of it, she was engaged to her best mates brother. They had been friends for some, time then started to date. Sally was 22 years old, and her boyfriend was 24, they were so in love.
Sally would play the lads up, dance with a few, have a laugh with them, sometimes a quick drink, but that was it. She never got tempted to stray, she enjoyed her job at the Queens, she worked in the foyer some nights and in the cloak room others, but Thursday night was her dance night with Vince. Vince was cool, never got flustered, when any of the guys on the dance floor got gobby,

"when you going to play this record or that record", "put a slow one on so I can dance close with my bird" he was your typical DJ smooth and cool.

Thursday was Vince's only night on stage but plays most lunchtimes 12-2. He was the maintenance man for the Queens in the daytime, but he loved working Thursday nights with Sally (no, nothing there, just good friends).

Alphonse pulled Steve into his office Thursday night, "sit down, let's have a chat," says Alphonse.

"What's up?" says Steve thinking, *what's all this about?*

"Just work," says Alphonse, "right, all bar managers must go on a first aid course, its compulsory. It's a five-day course and starts in two weeks time at the St Johns Ambulance in Solly Oaks."

"Well, who's going to run the bar when I'm away then?" says Steve, all worked up and looking at Alphonse as if he was going to hit him.

"Calm down Steve," says Alphonse, "it's just a first aid course not the third world war, Clark can run the bar, he's more than capable, yes?"

"Bloody poof," says Steve, "always sticking his nose in where its not wanted."

"Oh, come on Steve," says Alphonse, "stop being so bloody bolshy, it's not up for discussion, you do, or you don't, and if you don't, you get the bloody sack, its company policy for all bar managers to go on these courses, so just get on with it." he sees Steve to the door.

"Ok Clark, it's all set up, Steve's going on a first aid course so let's sort out the bar." says Alphonse, "on Thursday night, no fucking mistakes, we must make sure there's not cash missing, but if there is, well some ones for it, but keep quiet Clark, no telling the bar staff."

The dance floor was buzzing, Vince had just played this week's number one in the charts, it was a fast tune, and everyone was shouting play it again.
Nosy Parker and his mate Laughter were having a great time bopping to this tune, tonight they were dancing with two different partners, Nosy's was a polish girl, her name was very hard to pronounce so they called her Anita Chesty Cough as she was always coughing. Laughter's partner was a black girl, and she had these big tits, so they called her coconuts. She was a great bopper and when she was dancing all the lads would stand around and look at her tits, they were here, there, and everywhere.

At this time there were five girls who would stand in the middle of the dance floor and dance in sequence, they were all from Mary Tams dance school, not far from the Queens. All these girls were trained in all aspects of dance, they were not full time, it was two nights a week and Saturday mornings. These girls were mates and loved going to the Queens on Thursdays to show off in front of the rest of the crowd, they looked good, they all wore striped dresses and had good figures and plenty of admirers.
You could stand there all night and just look and learn, every guy and girl were doing something different, they all had their own way of dancing, it was a great way to meet new people.

Tonight, Sally was looking great, she danced and sang to all the records, she was fit. After a while she went to the bar for a drink, Clark served her and said, "Sally, how would you like to do me a big favour?" As usual, Sally was only too pleased to help, "yes, fire away." she said. Clark then takes Sally to a table and sits her down,

"right, ok Sally," says Clark, "Pam in the restaurant is really down, Steve's been playing his games again."
"What do you mean, after the birds again?" says Sally.
"Yes, he's just a big wanker." says Clark, looking at Sally as if to say *what can we do to help*. Sally says she will go and talk to Pam and cheer her up.
"Hi Pam, fancy a drink then? I see you're pretty quiet." says Sally.
"Yes ok" said Pam looking as if she was about to cry. They both sat down and Pam poured her heart out to Sally, marriage is like an operation, its ok till the bloody anaesthetic wears off, "I'm at a point where I'm ready to fuck him off, I cant catch him at it, but I know like everyone else does that Steve's a player, and when I do catch him then he'll wish he'd never met me, but I'll make sure he'll never forget me!" then off she goes back to the kitchen thanking Sally for her concern.

The next two weeks were hectic, always full most nights, everyone at the Queens knew they had to do their job 100% or Alphonse would jump on them. Steve was not happy going on this first aid course, he said the bar was far too important and him not being there would only make things more difficult for the staff, but Alphonse was not having any of it and told Steve to get his act into gear and get the fuck out.
Steve says he can still do the bar at night, not a problem he says, he was now worried the accountants were on to him, but Alphonse would not give way. So, Steve was now off for a week and Clark was running things. Every night Clark would make sure the tills were cashed up properly, he checked them on a regular basis and every night they were spot on, Alphonse was pleased but said they still could not prove Steve was the perpetrator, but Clark says when Steve comes back, he will mark all the

notes in the tills and then ask everyone to empty their pockets out at the end of the night. "Oh, this sounds too easy," says Alphonse.
"It's ok," Clark says smiling, "I've already had a word with the staff, they know the form."
"You've what?" says Alphonse, "what the hell are you playing at Clark? You just can't do that; you should have passed it by me!"
"Yes, well I just have." said Clark.
"Oh god, I hope this works Clark," said Alphonse, "or me and you are on our bikes! Well, not me, probably just you ha!" Alphonse wasn't going to commit himself to the dastardly deed, not just yet. If it works then he'll say that he set it all up, if it fails, nothing to do with him.
Steve returned to work and the first thing he says to Clark was, "were the tills ok? did they cash up ok?"
"Well, some nights they did, but a couple of nights they were short, but nothing to worry about." Clark says, as if there was no problem, Steve would think there's someone else at it, *fuck em' I'll still take mine then*. He's also glad as it doesn't look like its him (of course, there wasn't any cash missing, it was all a set up by Clark and Alphonse) so when Alphonse says to Steve that Clark will help check the tills just for this week, just to give him more practice for when Steve is on holiday, there wasn't any problem with Steve.

All the tills had this dye put in the draws, so when any notes were put under a light the dye would show up. The first night the tills were spot on, Steve knew it wasn't a good idea to nick anything the first night, so by Wednesday, Clark and Alphonse were worried that Steve had smelt a rat, and their plan was fucked so to speak. Then bingo, the tills were down by five pounds, Steve says to Clark this sort of thing happens and as its not too much cash missing, lets just put it down to experience. *Not bloody likely* thinks Clark, and calls Alphonse to the bar, "there are some problems with the tills, they don't add up correctly, there seems to be five pounds short." Steve says again that it's not a problem and they were all over reacting, "so, I'm pulling rank as the bar manager and asking you all to go home, ok?" "Pulling rank?" says Alphonse, "I'm the fucking general manager and I'm pulling rank, now everyone empty your pockets, come on, empty them."

The bar staff knew what the set up was and had no problem about emptying their pockets, but Steve says what's that going to prove, how can they tell who's got cash they shouldn't have? Steve was the last to empty his pockets, he had six pound notes and some change, Alphonse got the torch out of his coat and started to shine it on all the cash the bar staff had put on the counter, it was all clear no dye, then it was Steve's turn. And yes, every one the torch shone on showed up red dye, Alphonse looked at Steve and said, "you bloody thieving bastard, I knew you were at it!"

"What do you mean?" Steve says, looking all innocent. "Don't give me that," says Alphonse, then proceeds to explain to Steve how the tills were set up.

Yes, Steve was caught bang to rights.

Steve says Clark has set him up, "Oh, well how do you explain the notes in your pocket then?" Alphonse says looking daggers at Steve, "and the dye on them? You're just history, now get out of here, I'll talk to the boss's tomorrow, now good night."

Alphonse then explains to Pam about what's gone on in detail, he made sure she clearly understood what had happened. Pam's not too concerned about Steve, she is ready to boot him out at home, their love affair is over as far as she is concerned, END OF.

Next day Steve is asked to come to the Queens to talk about his job, Steve thinks he can fool Alphonse and keep his job. He walks into Alphonse's office full of himself, holding out his hand he says to Alphonse, "come on Sid, how long have we known each other? let's not spoil our relationship over a silly mistake shall we?"
"The names Alphonse, and what silly mistake are you talking about?"
Steve right away thinks Alphonse has decided to drop the whole thing, how wrong Steve was.
"There's no silly mistake," says Alphonse, "just downright bloody thieving, and you were caught bang to rights, now sit down and listen to what I've got to say."
Steve knew then his time was up, he just sat down and looked at Alphonse and said, "if there's any way, I can put this right, I will. I'll do anything you say."
"Oh, will you?" says Alphonse shaking his head, "such as?"
"Well," said Steve, "let Clark run the bar, and I'll just work as a barman, ok? I need this job, please give me a chance."
Alphonse just sat there and looked Steve right in the eyes, it lasted a few seconds. Steve was uncomfortable, then Alphonse spoke, "you say you'll do anything, well how about paying back the cash you stole over the year for a start?"
"What do you mean over the year? You think I'm responsible for all the missing money? Well how fucking dare you! can you prove that?" Said Steve.

"Last night was a start," says Alphonse, "and before I ring the police, I suggest you come clean and make things easy on yourself."

"Ring the police? oh no please Alphonse," says Steve, "no police!" Steve's now crying. Alphonse knows he's got Steve just where he wants him, "ok," he says, "put pen to paper and make a full statement to the bosses and I'll think about it."

"Ok, ok." says Steve, he's willing to do that, "then what happens to me?" he says.

"Just get writing Steve, then we'll discuss you." says Alphonse, and leaves Steve to make his statement and goes for a coffee in the restaurant. Pam's there of course but Alphonse is ready for her, "ok Pam, please join me for a coffee." he says. They both sit there, Pam's waiting to see what Steve had to say to Alphonse, "he's making a full statement," says Alphonse, "so it looks like the end for him as far as the Queens is concerned."

"Will he get arrested then?" asks Pam.

"I'll see what the statement reads like then ring head office and take it from there. What did Steve say last night when he got home?" says Alphonse to Pam.

"Not a bloody lot, just that Clark had set him up. But that Alphonse just fucks him off, I'm so pissed off with him, I've told him to get his kit together and leave the house, I want him out of my life sooner rather than later." then Pam excuses herself and goes about her business.

Alphonse walks back into his office, Steve has finished writing his statement, he has admitted everything. Alphonse sacks him there and then, "just get out of here," he said, "and I'll make sure any job you apply for, they know about your bloody thieving."

Steve leaves the Queens and walks down the front steps, then turns around to look back, *what a prat I've been* he thinks to himself and walks down the road crying. Pam had gotten rid of Steve, he ended up in a bedsit and worked in an old pub out of town just collecting glasses and cleaning up. He tried for a few jobs, but Alphonse was true to his word, everyone who rang the Queens for a reference got the full monty, Steve's a thief he does the tills don't trust him.

The Queens is once again full of drama, but its still the place to be and be seen, Well done Clark.

CHAPTER SIX

Wednesday night was strictly ballroom, and tonight the dance team are in the semi finals of the Midlands, all comers open, it's the top dance contest around Birmingham. Tonight, they have drawn a home tie, and guess what, they've drawn the British Legion, the old enemy. What a night this promises to be, the local TV station are covering the contest, so there's extra pressure on everyone in the contest. Alphonse is all fired up for this one, if the team get to the finals its another feather in his cap, the Queens is the biggest dance hall around Birmingham and always in the news, which Alphonse wants, but for the right reasons, no bad publicity. But "all publicity is good" says Mecca's bosses, well that depends on weather Alphonse is on the wrong end of it.

Anyway, tonight the spotlight is on the dance team and Jockstrap, oh yes, the one-legged wonder is the boss tonight. He's got to get his team ready for the contest, you might think its all done and dusted, they have been practicing all week, so what's Jock got to do tonight? A bloody lot, and much more. When the team arrive they are all ready to go to war, ready to show the opposition they mean business, you're messing with the Queens Empire mate so watch it! All of this is fine, until they get changed in the dressing room, then their nerves click in and it's "oh my god I'm shaking like a leaf!" "My legs have turned to jelly", "Oh bloody hell I want a shit", yes, we all get it, stomach churning, feeling sick, stage fright, this is where Jockstrap comes in, and of course the obligatory bottle of whiskey (scotch of course). One large scotch works wonders, one more and your fucked though, so it's one and only one. Then it's wind-up time, Jock is good at this, he knows who to bollock and who to sweet talk, who to pat on the back and who to kick up the arse, but most of all it's a team effort, and they don't forget that.

He's done a good job since Ann and Bert passed on, they would be proud of him and his wife. Jockstrap never forgot Ann and Bert and made sure the team didn't, on every team talk Jockstrap would always say Ann and Bert would do it this way or that way, but always said its me now and with Ann and Bert's guidance, I'll make you champions.
Tonight, the Queens was sweltering, it was full, there were the usual crowd who came every week, they loved to dance ballroom, it didn't matter whether they were any good or not, it didn't matter if they knew all the steps, they just loved ballroom. Tonight, they had the added excitement of the contest and the TV cameras, the amazing costumes, all the glitter and glam. So apart from the usual crowd, there were the people who just wanted to see the TV cameras and hopefully get a shot of themselves on TV. Then of course were the supporters from the British Legion, the Queens was rammed to the hilt, so full, the head doormen had to put extra men on the front doors to stop anymore coming in. Some guys and girls from the rock crowd were there just to take the piss, there's only rock and roll as far as they were concerned, but they had heard the dance team were doing the American jive tonight, so they were going to have some fun. You know, what's the bloody point of doing the jive, it's a young persons dance and most of the Queens team were over sixty and overweight. That was what all the youngsters thought, how wrong they were, and about to find out.
Alphonse was on form, best monkey suit, hair done to perfection, pure white shirt, dickie bow, the bloody lot.

Yes, Sir Alphonse Bouffant at your service, the general manager of the Queens Empire, the best dance hall in the city, best dance team, the best band, the best staff, and the best place to be.

The Bullring was buzzing with excitement, it's not very often you get the TV cameras in the Bullring at night, not in the early sixties anyway, but tonight they were. The crew were interviewing the locals to see what they thought of the dance contest. "Excuse me sir, a few words for our cameras?"
"Yes ok" says this guy.
"What do you think of the dance contest at the Queens tonight?"
"Oh yeah, its bloody ballroom ain't it, load of crap as far as I'm concerned mate! Rock and roll all the way, let's have a contest for that!" and walks off, ask a silly question!
"I think it's great mate" says this tramp pushing his way to the front of the crowd that had gathered, "I think ballroom is just tops, was that ok mate?" says the tramp, "give us a few pence for a cup of tea mate?"
"Oh, push off" the interviewer said, pushing the tramp to the side.
"Push off yourself mate!" said the tramp, "I've forgot more about ballroom than you've had hot dinners, I'm the one and only king of the two-foot shuffle, danced under London bridge in the war, danced for king and queen for two hours,"
"Ok, ok," said the interviewer, "where did you dance for the king then?"
"Saturday night, 1948, Queens Arms, Hall Green. Wednesday night, Kings Arms, 1949, now give us a few bob mate ha." The camera man pulled the tramp to one

side and gave him two and six and told him to piss off, yes, the Bullring was full of it tonight.

Clark was sweating blood, the bars were just heaving, the bar staff were run off their feet. "Two pints of bitter mate", "gin and tonic love", "bottle of stout and a bag of crisps" and so on, everyone wanted to be served first, it was none-stop, this is what its about, full throttle no time for smoking, no tea breaks, just keep the customers happy (well most of them).
"What do you mean I've short-changed you?" said one of the bar staff to a punter.
"I gave you a five," said the punter, "and you've given me change for two quid!" There was always someone who would try it on when the bars were busy, but the staff were just the best, they were trained to put all paper money on top of the till, then take out the change, then put the notes in the till, all professional, not much got past them.

The restaurant was also full, mainly because you could see the whole of the dance floor from up there, some just had a snack, most had a full meal. It was so exciting just watching the dancing never mind being on the dance floor. The sixties was the most exciting time for music and fashion, everything was changing from the forties and fifties, which was mostly crooners and ballads, more freedom for women, the pill and all that, mini skirts, shorter hair styles, more and more girls were being open about what they wanted to do, you know sex, drink, dress, going out with the girls, getting better jobs, it was all about being seen. The older guys loved all this in their younger days, there was none of this stuff going on, it was more than some girls life if they were late home or came home drunk, their mothers or fathers would sort them out, "don't bring shame on our house", "get to bed, you're not going out again this week", but now the swinging sixties were here, almost anything went. It was life changing for a lot of people and didn't they just love it? The streets in the city centre were full of people going or coming from somewhere, there were lots of parties, lots of clubs, life was just one big party for some people. There were plenty of jobs around, you could have two jobs in one day, no CV's needed, "can you do this?", "Yes, I can", "ok start straight away". There was plenty of building work about, new shopping centres being built, twelve story blocks of flats, office blocks, all these new projects led to other work, plenty of factories and black smoke to go with them, that's why they called it the Black Country.

It was a good time for everything, music, work, and free love, well perhaps not with the local prostitutes, that would cost you a pound or two, plenty of coppers on the beat and you didn't have to wait two days for them to turn up when you rang the police station. Like everything else in the swinging sixties, there was plenty of fun, dance halls in every street, pubs buzzing, coffee bars swinging, new music, new singers, "what's all this Elvis about then? the dad's would say to their kids, "looks like a poof to me", if you didn't like the sixties, you didn't like life itself.

Jockstrap had got his team together in the dressing room, everyone was changed into their dancing costume, everyone got changed in the same room, no one worried about being seen in their knickers or underpants, that's if anyone had them on at all, you just got on with it. All the girls' hair was neat and tidy, they had all had it done that day, most of the men as well, you had to look your best on these nights, The ladies dresses were beautiful, sequined and all the same colour, the men wore dress suits with dickie bows, it was a real treat to see them come onto the dance floor all in line, all in step, and not a hair out of place. But for now, it was time to just reflect on what they had practiced on their afternoon sessions at the Queens.

Jockstrap was going through all the dance routines, all the team were very attentive, this was a big night for them all, their friends and family were there, there was a lot at stake. Nobody wanted to make any mistakes, as was said before, it was squeaky bum time for them all. Nearly time to go out on the dance floor, both teams come out together at the start and are introduced to the judges and audience. Then the host team, which tonight is the Queens, starts first. But before this Jockstrap has to wind everyone up, "remember the war, that fighting spirit!" he always mentioned the bloody war, "if the British Legion think they can beat us they must be bloody mad! We are the best team in the Midlands, we don't need to beat them, they must beat us, we are just too good for them, they will try hard. As for us, just do the thing we're good at, that's good old bloody dancing, and help each other if someone forgets their steps, so come on, lets show the TV cameras what we are made of, and most of all, smile all the time", everyone was now ready and out they go to the cheers of the Queens crowd. The sound was almost deafening, the TV commentator was announcing the two teams and telling everyone how good they looked, and they did, both teams were dressed just beautifully, and they looked a treat, all in line bowing to the judges and the crowd. Alphonse was standing by the stage, he looked like he was going to cry, he was so proud of the team, they had come a long way, he really wanted them to do well for themselves. Never mind the Queens, they were a good bunch of people, never any trouble (except for Tilly's pipe) so his fingers and toes were crossed for them. The band had their music all sorted and were ready to get things moving.

The British Legion left the floor, everything went quiet, the Queens team were ready for their first dance, they had to dance three collectively, and then two couples on their own, then the judges had to score points for all the dances and tell the teams where they had gone wrong (well if they had) or how well they had done.
The band struck up and away the team went, all in step, all smiling, twirling heads to the right, heads to the left, they had worked hard on their afternoon sessions, and by God did it show. They were brilliant, their three dances as a team were worth watching, and did the crowd applaud them, their hands must be hurting.
Now it was just the two couples, Jockstrap and his wife and Tilly and her husband, they were the best individual dancers in the team, you wouldn't have guessed it with Tilly, she was big and so was her husband Rupert, but they were good dancers as most of the Caribbean people were, and tonight was no different, they were fantastic. So was Jockstrap and his wife, it was worth the two-bob paid to come in tonight, even the young rockers were in awe of them. "Don't they look good doll?" says a guy to his bird.
"Yes," she said, "shall we take up ballroom?"
"Don't be daft," he replies, "we would look really naff in them costumes." Well, it takes all sorts, but tonight it's strictly ballroom.
All dances over for the Queens team, they had a good score and a good response from the judges, Jockstrap

was really pleased and so was Alphonse, *beat that* he thought to himself, it's the best he'd seen the team dance. He takes a tray of drinks into the dressing room and congratulates them, "we haven't won yet" says Jockstrap, "but yes I do agree with you, we were great." On to the dance floor walks the British Legion, they also look great, and they were just as good as the Queens, and the crowd cheered and clapped them with the same enthusiasm. This was going to the wire, there wasn't much to choose between the two teams, as at the final score it was 20 points each.

"Oh god, a dance off" says Jockstrap, this is when the judges pick what dance they want the two teams to perform, it could be a team effort or just one couple from each team, tonight it was one couple from each team, and it was the American Jive. They didn't have to do the jive as a team, which they thought they had to, the judges decided to leave it out, but if there was a dance off, then it would be on.

"Ha, ha that's us fucked!" say the young rockers, "who's going to do that? These lot are all over the top ha." *Oh, ye of little faith, lets show you what ballrooms all about.*

"Ladies and gentlemen," says the compare, "tonight it's a dance off, and the first couple on the dance floor are from the British Legion." Everyone applauded them and off they went. They were good, oh God they were.

"Oh well, we tried hard," says Jockstrap, "you can't win them all can you?"

"What?" says Tilly, "we'll show them what it's all about!" puffing on her pipe. It was Tilly and Rupert who were doing the jive (what? you must be joking). They were the best in the team at the jive, so here goes.

Onto the floor walks Tilly and Rupert, "what the bloody hell are they doing?" say the young rockers, "they're doing the jive? you must be joking! its no contest, lets go to the bar for a drink."

"No hang on, let's just see what they have got." says his girl.

"Oh, ok, if you must" he replies.

Looking at Tilly and Rupert you wouldn't have given them much of a chance, they were both big, the two from the British Legion were only young, and knew whoever their rivals were, they had to work hard as they were really good, young, fit, and full of spunk.

Tilly was fourteen stone and Rupert was sixteen stone, although he was not fat, just big built. Tilly was slightly on the fat side, so everyone was just looking at each other thinking "they've got no chance, there just too big for the jive". Alphonse just couldn't see why Jockstrap had picked these two, *oh well never mind we did our best* thought Alphonse. But Jockstrap knew what he was doing.

Tilly and Rupert stood in front of the judges holding hands, there were no nerves at all, the judges were thinking *are these the best the Queens have got? They will have to go some to beat the British Legion.* Tilly turns to face Rupert, the dance hall is very quiet, the band strikes up full blast, "let's go" says Tilly to Rupert, "let's show these bastards what the jive is all about", then winks at Jockstrap, then off they go all round the dance floor. Tilly swinging to the right of Rupert then to the left, they were fucking brilliant. It was like watching two teenagers, so full of energy, their legs were moving like the speed of light, all around the dance floor. Rupert was swinging Tilly all over the place, it was electrifying to watch. The young rockers were just mesmerized, they had never seen anything like this, ever. How could Tilly and Rupert keep this up, it was so fast. They had just two minutes to do the jive, but that's a long time at this speed, then suddenly Tilly and Rupert faced each other, Tilly ran at Rupert, he bent his knee's and lifted Tilly over his head. *Bloody hell!* everyone thought, but Tilly was ok, she landed on her feet just like an Olympic Athlete. The crowd went ballistic, this was like a moment in life when you think *where was I on so and so date? Oh yes at the Queens watching Tilly and Rupert dancing the American jive*, yes, it was that good. Rupert then turned to face Tilly, she then ran at him, he caught her arms and threw her through his legs then turned and caught her arms and lifted her up. She then somehow did a somersault and landed in front of the judges with Rupert by her side. *Fucking beat that!* thought Tilly.

The dance finished, the judges were on their feet and clapping, never been known before. Jockstrap just stood there; he's never ever seen anything like this before, how the bloody hell did they do that? Alphonse didn't know what to say to Jockstrap, he knows that was a winner, by God it was. The judges scored 10, 10, 10, 10, full house, the young couple who were their opponents just stood there in awe. The Queens were through to the final, "oh God thank you, thank you!" says Jockstrap. Tilly then took Rupert's hand and walked over to the plaque on the wall at the end of the dance floor, it's the plaque in memory of Bert and Ann, Tilly jumps onto a table so she can reach the plaque, she kisses her hand, then puts her hand on the plaque, and says to herself, *the pipe did come in useful Ann at the end, God bless.* Yes, we know what Tilly's talking about don't we? Let's just keep that to our selves for now shall we, thanks.

Alphonse was almost hoarse he had been shouting for Tilly and Rupert, "right this calls for a drink!" then off to the bar he almost ran, "Clark, one large scotch please." He put a fiver on the bar, "better make that two son, old Jockstrap's on his way over… here get that down your throat."

"Are you happy?" says Jockstrap to Alphonse.

"Happy? you bet your life I'm happy! Well done to you and your team, and that last dance, well how the bloody hell did they do that for God's sake?"

"Oh, they have special herbs they take that makes them more flexible."

"Special herbs?" says Alphonse, "well make sure they have some next week, as its Gala night."

"Well, that's rock night" says Jockstrap.

"Yes," says Alphonse, "and I want our dance team on the bloody floor that night, show the young dudes what its all about, especially Tilly and Rupert they fucking rock for England."

And with that they both drank their drinks and Jockstrap went to the dressing room to enjoy their win over the old enemy, and with a bottle of scotch for the team to enjoy from Alphonse, bless him.

CHAPTER SEVEN

Gala night was a fantastic night at the Queens, there was so much going on, dance competitions, beauty competitions, free and easy (singing with the band for anyone that fancied themselves) and prizes, prizes, prizes. Alphonse had got a good budget for gala night, so anyone who entered any of these competitions had a chance of winning a good prize, so what a good night this was going to be. These were fantastic nights, it was a good time to be around, stop in and watch TV, or stop in and have sex, none of this sky TV and sixty channels, just three then. So, Saturday nights were exceptional, you worked all the week and come Saturday, you're ready for some fun. In the sixties the city centres were full of people, it was like there was a football match on, people everywhere, hundreds and hundreds of them all going to their favourite dance hall, pubs, or clubs. The atmosphere was electric, all dressed in their best suits or dresses, the dress code for the early sixties for men was mainly Italian suits (funny they're back on the scene again). The girls, well their dresses got shorter as the years went by, the mini was the best dress that was ever invented, that's a fact, well tell me what guy would disagree?

To the young lads who it was their first time in the city centre on a Saturday night, there's only one word for it, FABULOUS. Their eyes were everywhere, "look at her", "look at him", "oh this is bloody great mate, I hope this lasts for ever." For the girls it was, "I hope I look ok", "he's looking at me ain't he", or "she looks a tart in that outfit", I think it's the same now, isn't it?
In the pubs the talk was what's on at the Queens tonight, or they were already going there and met in the pub to

have a drink and plan their night, or which bird they were going after. Not many girls used the pubs then, not like today, there were plenty of pubs that would not allow women in the bar at all, they could go in the smoke room or assembly room, and some landlords were very strict on the age limit. "Are you old enough to drink son? how old are you?"
"I'm eighteen mate." (They always said eighteen never nineteen or twenty).

So you might think, what's so good about the swinging sixties then? Just think, three or four years ago there was never the freedom the young people got in the sixties, you had to be in at eight thirty at night even when you were sixteen. Of course there were the young rogues who wouldn't be, but when you're sat at home at night and all you listen to is the crooners, (Frank Sinatra, Bing Crosby and so forth) then all of a sudden, there was rock and roll, Elvis, Jerry Lee Lewis, Bill Haley, Little Richard, all rocking and saying, "come on kids let yourself go, lets rock and roll!" It was like being let out of a straight jacket, even some of the moms and dads let themselves go, to the embarrassment of their kids, weddings, birthdays, family get togethers, mom and dad always said, "lets show them how it's done." (Come on, I think we've all been through that at some time or another).

So, Saturday night was a goer for most. Alphonse had extra staff on, must keep everything flowing smoothly. Pam had got herself a new assistant, a man of about thirty-five years old and from Devon. He had been working for Mecca for some time, but the boss's said he needed to work in a bigger environment to get more experience, as he wanted to be a general manager. He and Pam got on well, when Pam got feisty, he would calm her down, so it worked well. It got to the point where there were rumours, they were seeing each other after work, Pam was now a free agent, she had got rid of Steve and the divorce was going through, so what's the problem?

The Queens was open at 7 o'clock tonight, and it soon filled up, all the tables around the dance floor were full, everyone wanted to be near the action, they didn't want to miss a thing, and there's going to be plenty to see tonight.
"Hey, Alphonse, what's with the ballroom geezers tonight then?" shouted a guy by the bar, "I thought it was rock night?"
"Wait and see my son, and don't put them down, they might come back and haunt you!"
"Oh yeah" says this guy, "have they come to learn how to rock then?" Alphonse looked at the lad and thought *yes, I'll get Tilly to put him through his paces, then we'll see who's got to learn.*
Alphonse knew he would get some stick tonight, but he wasn't worried, he'd seen the dance team perform, so no worries there.

Terry was the compare tonight, and the dance band were ready to rip the place apart, there was also some records played by the DJ.
Alphonse had warned Terry no fucking tricks tonight, and no cock ups, have some fun but keep our reputation intact or you'll have me to deal with. Terry was fine, he would always charm the girls, but tonight, no raffle ticket scams.
Jockstrap was sitting with the rest of the dance team in the upstairs bar, where you could look down on the

dance floor. "Bloody mad crowd," he said to his mate, "they call this the best night of the week, they're so loud!"
"Oh, shut up and have another drink," says his wife, "let's just enjoy the night, we might learn something tonight" winking at her mate.

"Ladies and gentlemen," said Terry through the mic, "shall we get the party started?" The crowd just went wild, "yes come on!" they all shouted, the band started with the number one in the charts, a good loud rock number. The dance floor soon filled up, with bodies shaking, twisting, and jumping, oh my god what a sight it was, no one worried how they looked, they were just enjoying themselves. This is what Saturday nights were all about, the band played three or four numbers, they had a guy and a girl singing, they sang separately and together, everyone loved them. Tonight, Sally was also dancing on stage, so it was the full commitment of the dance staff, well its Gala night, nothing is too much for the customers.

Terry says "shall we have our first competition? its rock and roll, come on who's up for it? Let's have the couples on the dance floor, shall we?" The dance floor cleared, then the first couple came on followed closely by the next and soon there were about twenty couples on the floor, Tilly looked at Rupert as if to say, *shall we?* Jockstrap said, "no Tilly, save it for later" and winked at her.

The band struck up and the floor was in a frenzy, there were some great dancers on the floor tonight, Nosy Parker was one of them, tonight he was with his regular girlfriend Tina, she was a good looker and a good dancer, she also liked to show her knickers, and the lads loved to see them. The judges soon got it down to four couples. "Ok," says Terry, "let's have a rest for five minutes and have a song from one of our great singers." This gives the last four couples time to recuperate. With the song over, "let's have you lot on the floor" says Terry, "and may the best couple win!" And off they go, it was just magic to watch, they were all good, but there can only be one winner. There was no 1st 2nd and 3rd it was just one winner and that's it. A girl and boy from Sheldon won it, they were only sixteen but very good. "And the next dance please" says Terry (well that's what they said in those days) everybody sits down and has a drink and a chat, next was the beauty contest. Terry loved this, all these lovely birds, *oh my god, which one do I fancy* he thought, *no, no Alphonse said no fucking ducking and diving tonight let's have a straight vote*, *right she's great*, and *oh she's brilliant*, and *look at her tits! Oh, fuck* thinks Terry *they are all winners.*

Tonight's judges are ones from the local rag, Susan French from the biggest hairdressers in Birmingham and Tommy Thomas the manager of Birmingham City football club. There are quite a few girls in the contest tonight, some had come from Wolverhampton and some from Coventry, it was a big night for all the girls, win this and it would build for bigger things, so it was important to look good and say the right thing. All the girls paraded around the dance floor, there certainly was some nice-looking girls, the lads in the crowd called and whistled them as they walked around, "hey stop that you crazy guys!" shouted Terry laughing, "we might have a lads contest next!" (he'd love that).
The girls were each asked a question, you know, what would you do if you won the contest? Or what's your life's ambition? Or what time does the news at ten come on? (Well, some are dumb as well as pretty) one girl

said, "if I win tonight, I will ask my boyfriend to marry me", then someone shouts from the back of the dance floor, "oh Christ make sure she loses!"
"Ha!" Terry says, *is that her boyfriend then?* Then the girl from Wolverhampton says if she wins, she would like to go into TV and be a news presenter, (*what with that bloody Black Country accent, you must be joking* Terry thinks to himself).

It was all good fun and no harm done, all the girls were just great, they all had their photos taken and it was front page news in the B-ham rag next night.
The winner came from Hagley, in Birmingham, she won a holiday for two, and was entered into the Miss England contest at Butlins Skegness.
The night was going fine, everyone was up for a good night and currently, no one was disappointed.
Alphonse had told Jockstrap to get the team together and he would introduce them to the crowd, and then ask them to do the American jive. The dance team stood just at the side of the stage, Alphonse took the mic off Terry and introduces the team and says what a great team they had at the Queens. The crowd gave them a good response, "ok boys and girls, take it away" says Alphonse, and the team go straight into the jive. And what a good job they did, they were just fabulous, no one could fault them, most of the crowd just stood in amazement, the rest clapped to the music. Alphonse noticed the lad who had questioned him at the bar was standing just by the side of the dance floor, "hey son, fancy a try with one of our dance team?" The lad turned white, "not a bloody chance!" he said, "they're so good, sorry for what I said earlier on". *Yes, you fucking loser*, Alphonse thought, then disappeared. The dance team

had won the Saturday night crowd over, yes mate they're part of the Queens Empire, you bet they are.

There was a short break so everyone could get their breath back, Terry comes on stage, "well what did you think of that then?" he said, "well done to our dance team" then Terry puts his hands up, "please, let's have some quiet, come on shush, right boys and girls, we all know Alphonse our general manager don't we yes? And he likes to boss us about, well how about him showing us how it's done then?" Everybody looks at each other, *what's he mean? Can he dance as well as boss us about, can he, come on, can he?* The crowd respond and start calling for Alphonse to appear, "well where is he?" says Terry winding the crowd up. Then suddenly, the lights are turned up and standing at the top of the stairs leading to the dance floor stood Alphonse and Pam. Alphonse was out of his monkey suit and in jeans and trainers, a flowered shirt and looked a million dollars. Pam was dressed the same but in different colours. *What's all this about then?* everyone thought it was a joke, "oh fuck, he can't dance, can he?" they were all saying to each other. This has got to be a joke.

Alphonse puts his hand up to signal that he and Pam are ready, Terry says "well what have we here then? I was only joking boss, but if you like you can carry on" and he walked off stage. Of course, it was all set up wasn't it, Pam and Alphonse have been put through their paces by Jockstrap and his wife for the last few weeks, and they are ready to show the young ones how its done, oh I hope so for their sake.

Pam and Alphonse walk to the middle of the dance floor, everything goes quiet, the crowd hold their breath, Alphonse's heart is beating ten to the dozen, and he whispers to Pam, "what have we let ourselves in for?" Pam says, "it's too late now so lets go" then looks Alphonse in the eyes as if to say, *let me down and I'll kick your bollocks in.* The band plays the tune the dance team danced to, and off Pam and Alphonse went. To say they were good was an understatement, they were bloody amazing. Pam was fantastic, she looked as if she had been dancing all her life, and Alphonse, well what can one say but brilliant, they never put a foot wrong at all. They jived their way all around the dance floor, at one point Alphonse jumped into the air, then did the splits, don't ask me how but he did it like a professional. They both surpassed themselves and when they finished, they had a standing ovation for two minutes. The band joined in with the applause, Terry just stood there in amazement, Jockstrap was proud of them, Clark was crying, Pam was waving to everyone, and Alphonse, he was fucked, but he got through it, like a pro he was (pissed and a little help from Tilly's peace pipe, keep it to yourselves).

Pam went back to the restaurant and didn't bother to get changed, she was on a high, though not as high as Alphonse. He got changed back into his monkey suit, then strode around the Queens as if nothing had happened. He and Pam won over the youngsters that night and were the talk of the town for weeks.

Back to the Gala night and there was a girl on stage singing a blues number, she was out of the crowd, it was free and easy time. She was good, and all the crowd clapped her when she finished. Next on was a young lad, he looked like butter wouldn't melt in his mouth, but could he sing and dance? you bet he could. These nights were magic, people often wonder if ever these nights would come back, but I'm afraid they are lost in the archives of our minds, they are once in a lifetime things that happen, and when we get older, we sit and dream about them and tell our children how it all started.

Butlins run sixties weekends now and again, everyone meets up, and all have a good time, but its not like the real thing. You know you were there when it all started, you walked into the Queens, there were big pictures of film stars on the walls as you walked to the dance floor, the smell of the Queens, not a nasty smell, a good old-fashioned smell of a good night in the making. Not much trouble, if any, just a good old time was had by all.

Alphonse was at the Queens for three and a half years, then moved back to London to run a hotel for Mecca, he got married and his wife helped him to run the hotel. He dropped the name Alphonse, he was just plain Sam now, he had been a good manager, and was always remembered when anyone talked about the Queens.
Terry stayed at the Queens until it closed, then he went on to compare on cruise liners.
Pam teamed up with the new guy who was there training to be a manager, they both moved to Devon and took over a pub come restaurant, they did well for themselves.
Clark, well he ended up running a big restaurant in London, but never forgot the Queens. He always got the customers attention by telling stories of the Queens.

Sadly, the Queens shut down after a few years and was turned into a bank, the front was kept the same with the big archways, so it was always remembered as a dance hall.

Jockstrap and the team moved to a club, no it wasn't the British Legion, they still danced the night away.
Some days you could see people stop outside the bank and look up at the archways and smile to themselves, yes, the good old Queens.
One Saturday, a gran and granddad were standing outside the bank with their two grandchildren, they were taking them to the burger bar for a treat, the grandma said "oh, the good old days love," looking at the granddad.
"Yes," he says, "rock and roll."
"What's rock and roll granddad?" says the young boy.
"Come on, let's have a burger and I'll try and tell you." They sit down and order their burgers, when the waitress brings them over, gran and granddad are telling their grandchildren about the Queens, "oh the Queens," says the waitress, "the good old days!" she says to grandma, "I've heard some stories about the Queens, all good," and looking at granddad she says, "would you do it all over again if you could?" Grandma looked at granddad and they both winked at each other. WHAT DO YOU THINK.

Printed in Great Britain
by Amazon